THE LAST TRAIN FROM BERLIN

Other Books by George Blagowidow

Operation Parterre
In Search of Lady Lion Tamer

THE LAST TRAIN FROM BERLIN

George Blagowidow

HIPPOCRENE BOOKS, INC.
New York

Hippocrene paperback edition, 1995.

For information, address:
HIPPOCRENE BOOKS, INC.
171 Madison Avenue
New York, NY 10016

Library of Congress Cataloging in Publication Data

Blagowidow, George.
The last train from Berlin.

I. Title.
PZ4.B6299Las [PS3552.L344] 813'.5'4
ISBN 0-7818-0368-3
Library of Congress Catalog Card Number 76-23749

Printed in the United States of America.

To Irene

"Then I grieved, and now I grieve again,
when I turn my mind to what I saw."

DANTE, *Inferno*

THE LAST TRAIN FROM BERLIN

CHARACTERS

Adam Leski—Known also as Heinz Hauptmann, high school student

Adolf Hitler—The Führer of the Third Reich

MACABR—A Gestapo unit in charge of protecting the Führer's life

Members of the Unit:

Rudolf Malec—*Obersturmbannführer* (Major)

Friedrich Cart—*Sturmbannführer* (Captain)

Wilhelm Bismar—*Hauptsturmführer* (Senior Lieutenant)

Dietrich Rüger—*Obersturmführer* (Lieutenant)

Heinrich Himmler—*Reichsführer,* the head of the SS and the Gestapo

Otto Harimann—Himmler's man for his secret schemes; also director of the *Oberschule*

Ferdinand Piersohn—A former teacher of English, at Harimann's disposal

Wolfgang Neufeind—Mathematics teacher, works with Piersohn

Else Bismar—Wife of *Hauptsturmführer* Bismar

Lilka Konarski—Adam's girl friend

Wacek Konarski—Her brother

Father Sebastian—A Catholic priest, also Adam's former teacher

Anton Kotecha—Nurse at the *Oberschule*

Andreas Wendel—Adam's friend

Stefan Wirski—Member of the Polish Underground

PROLOGUE

Saturday, November 7, 1942

The train, which was moving west now, was no ordinary collection of railroad cars. It was made up of twelve luxury cars, all of them recently built on special order. On each end was an armored car equipped with the most modern weapons, including antiaircraft artillery. All the windows were fitted with special, bulletproof glass and with retractable steel shutters that could be lowered at will to make each car as invulnerable as an armored tank.

In the dining car, dessert was being served to the four men seated around the damask-covered table. Three of the men were sipping cognac, but Hitler, as usual, refrained from this indulgence.

It was one of the most crucial moments of the war, with the German Sixth Army fighting in Stalingrad on a strenuously extended front, and other divisions waging battle in the Caucasus.

The Russian Army even now was preparing a counteroffensive. Hitler, who directed the conduct of the war in person, reserving the most vital decisions for himself, should have been at headquarters with his general staff. But personal motives had drawn him away. As all his dining companions knew, the Führer could seldom let six months go by without a visit to his hideaway in Berchtesgaden and his mistress, Eva Braun.

This time his pretext was the "necessity" of addressing his Party colleagues on the nineteenth anniversary of the Munich Putsch.

As the train halted in Posen, another train, also westbound, stopped beside it on a parallel track. This one was evacuating soldiers from the front, an assortment of weary, wounded, hungry men. At the sight of their Führer, these men did not cheer when they recognized the special train and its special occupant. Their only response to the sumptuous surroundings and the rich food on the tables was silence, backed by cold stares. For the first time in all his confrontations with his troops Hitler turned from their sight and directed the waiter to lower the shutters.

At 4 A.M. on November 8 the train, after a long stop at the station of Fulda, was cleared for departure. The next stop: Würzburg, a journey of about three hours.

As the Führer studied the map dotted with small towns between Fulda and Würzburg, his eyes stopped at one of the names: Sterbfritz. "*Die Fritz,*" it meant, or, symbolically, "die Germany." Slowly he retired to his bedroom compartment. An unpleasant thought.

There was nothing on the map to indicate that the same town some thousand years ago had been named Stark Frides, or "strong peace," acquiring its present meaning only through many word changes.

And there was nothing to indicate to him that over the exit of one of the tunnels between which the station of Sterbfritz lies, a man stood in silence, ready to jump on the Führer's train, to jump and to kill.

I

February 1940

Standing to attention, with their right hands raised, the seventeen boys repeated in unison:

"In the presence of this blood banner which represents our Führer I swear to devote all my energies and my strength to the savior of our country, Adolf Hitler. I am willing and ready to give up my life for him, so help me God."

The seventeen stood in a straight line, facing their teachers, those schoolmates who already had taken this Hitler Youth oath of allegiance, and the younger ones who were not yet allowed to. The snow-covered mountains around them echoed their words. The swastika armbands had been attached to their brown shirts only a few hours before. Standing there, they did not feel the cold wind, their eyes fastened on the large swastika with a portrait of Adolf Hitler in its center.

After the oath the boys began to sing the "*Horst Wessel*" song, each with his right hand raised in the Nazi salute.

Heinz Hauptmann, the third boy in the line of those taking the oath, did not join the others. The words he had just spoken lingered in his mind:

"All my energies and my strength . . . Adolf Hitler . . . I am willing and ready to give up my life . . . to take his life . . . so help me God."

Heinz failed to obey the command "*Rechts-um*" (right on) and had to be reminded by a colleague behind him. The boys then marched to the school building, where they were dismissed.

Since it was Sunday, those boys who were on good behavior, without any demerits or failing grades, could go to the town called Nyphelheim only four kilometers away. There they normally bought strudel and drank sweet ersatz coffee made from chicory and wheat. They were always hungry, although the school food was as good as it could be in wartime, that February of 1940. The diet was planned to build strong men to serve as soldiers for the Third Reich.

Heinz, who had arrived at the school only three weeks before, had not yet joined the rowdy groups that hung around the café and the bakery, never sated, singing and shouting, and pushing and punching each other along the road to Nyphelheim and back to the *Oberschule*. He was so thin that it seemed as if only his bare skin covered the square bone structure of his face, giving emphasis to the dark blue of his eyes under the blond hair.

"*Heimweh*," the housemaster explained, not unkindly. Homesickness. He had seen it before and knew the look of it. The cure was outdoor exercise, a heavy schedule of classes, long study hours, and brisk mountain outings with his comrades in the *Hitlerjugend*. The boy would come around. He was good at math and chemistry when he put his mind to it, and in spite of his rather slight build, champion material on the soccer field. Sullen temperament, the headmaster said, but it was just homesickness. "Be patient, Herr Direktor, and you will see."

The bell rang at six the next morning through the mountain air, and the boys spilled out to the drill yard for calisthenics. The air was frosty; snow covered the earth as far as the eye could see. When their blood was racing and their faces pink with exertion, the gymnastics teacher blew the whistle and they poured into the dining hall for coffee and bread.

Heinz's head was spinning from the cold and the exercise; he pushed his way through the door with a group of smaller boys and felt a sharp pinch on his thigh. "Animal!" he cursed mildly, not knowing which one did it. The younger boys tormented him because he was new, and had a Polish accent, and never fought back. He seemed to live within himself most of the time, not noticing them, though they constantly tried to make him lose his temper. He was accommodating but reluctant to be part of the group. He hadn't even got their names straight yet, and didn't care if they called him Heinrich or Holtz or Hermann in revenge for his mistakes. They called him Polak, too, and got a box in the ear for it from the housemaster if he heard them, for if a Pole were to be found in the school, its honor would be demeaned.

The first class, *Rassenkunde* (The Study of Races), started at eight o'clock, where Heinz learned painfully the traits that make a man better than his fellows—the mystical fluids, blood, bile, glandular secretions—the emanations that, cleansed and perfected by rite and mystery, had made the Nordic race godlike.

After class, two boys were discussing the subject of the preceding lecture. A fat smallish boy, named Andreas Wendel, asked the other in a worried voice:

"Did you get it? Is the Nordic race the best, Heinrich?"

The tall strong boy, with a thick neck the diameter of his head, nodded. "Sure it is, Andreas. The men of this race are courageous warriors and victors."

They were standing in the men's room and the taller boy was smoking a cigarette.

"But our Führer is not Nordic," said Andreas, pushing back his blond hair from his freckled forehead.

"You must have been asleep during the last class," said Heinrich. "The Führer combines the best traits of the Nordic, Westphalian, and the Alpine races."

"But if the Nordic race is the best, then the combination and mixture of other races is less than best?"

"The Führer is the best," said Heinrich.

Heinz, the new boy, was passing by and Andreas, who wanted to involve him in this conversation, asked:

"Why should we hate the Jews and Slavs, if some of them are Nordic?"

Heinz shrugged his shoulders.

"We in the Oberschule should not do that," said Heinrich. "Hatred is for the masses. We should expect that they will disappear."

"But why?" persisted Andreas.

The bell rang and the boys moved quickly to their next class. On the way, Heinrich continued his explanation. "Their souls and their bodies do not correspond. Remember the lecture about Gobineau's theory?"

Heinz wrote down the categories and significances of facial bone, skull height, muscle form and articulation, shape of brow and fingernail; he copied faithfully and neatly, so that the instructor would praise his diligence. But when called on in class he stuttered wrong answers, foolish syllables, half-Polish, half-jargon, until he would be asked mercifully to desist and get a failing grade for the day. Once, when asked to recite the characteristics of the various races that inhabit the former Poland, now the "General Gouvernement," he had run from the classroom and barely reached the hall before he vomited. He was chastened by two days of bitter purgatives administered by a rough old Czech medic, Anton Kotecha, a menial Slav like the flat-faced workmen who had appeared in the depths of January to make the roofs safe by shoveling down the heavy accumulation of snow. As he lay in bed, Heinz thought back to another humiliation. One day as he was standing by watching the workmen, one of them winked at him in comradely greeting. "Any ships on the horizon?" And "Have you sighted land yet?" he had shouted to them idly, to strengthen the fragile thread of sympathy. When they shrugged and turned away, he had repeated the jest in Polish, and crooked elfin smiles crossed their red faces. One of them tossed a shovelful of powdery snow down on his head and said, "Cannibal islands, *mein Herr*." Heinz had not understood his meaning. He was confined for two Sunday afternoons to the unheated mudroom where the boys cleaned their boots and kept miscellaneous pieces of sporting gear. He was instructed curtly by the housemaster that Germans demean themselves by jesting with persons of inferior races. Particularly dangerous was the use of a common language which might carry the inference that the inferiors' culture was an instrument meriting recognition. These men were fit to shovel the roofs, sweep streets, dispose of refuse, and clean latrines; one did not communicate with them.

Heinz took the lesson sourly, in its substance as well as in the form of its administration. In rebellion he chose an edition of Schopenhauer's aphorisms to read in his exile, because he fancied he could find in it a phrase he had once been told the dour philosopher had written: "The Germans are a stupid race."

"Stubborn and self-important" went down on his record in the secret file kept by Dietrich Rüger, the new instructor in charge of the Hitler Youth unit for upperclassmen. "Needs vigorous correction." A notation in the margin read "physical?" But capitulation, like a sound one cannot hear or a color beyond the spectrum, was out of Heinz's range.

When Heinz met Rüger for the first time, his reaction was that of instant repulsion. Linked with the feeling of repugnance, however, was the feeling that he had already seen this man whose whole bearing reflected the military. He struggled to retrieve the memory of the occasion on which he might have encountered Rüger, but it would not surface. After a while he forgot about that feeling from the past, although his antipathy for this vigorous but vainglorious man remained with him.

When the first thaw was in the air, Rüger announced a daylong snowshoe expedition into the mountains for a select group of senior boys (the school owned a limited number of pairs of snowshoes) to test their endurance and to prepare them for possible future service in the conquest of the East. They must be ready, he explained, to form part of the elite who would lead the great colonization soon to begin, once the eastern boundaries of the Reich were established and the Slavs subdued.

The choleric Rüger gave a stirring talk to the three senior classes gathered in the gym after the Saturday night study hour.

His narrow gray eyes gleamed like ice splinters under a cloudy sky. Certain of those present were to be the leaders of great migrations, he told them as though he were privy to the secrets of the Führer himself; they were to govern settlements of pure Germans in the territories now under the rule of the Russians. There were great plains there, fertile in summer with wheat, rye, barley, and fruit orchards. In the winter the snow covered them with life-generating dark, like the dark conjunction of man and woman that brings men into the world, to nourish, to subjugate, to rule.

Heinz was among those chosen to go on the trek; they were selected by lot, but it was evident from minute hesitations as Rüger read out the names drawn from a basket that he substituted those of boys he wanted. He tore up the lots as he read them and tossed the scraps into a basket with calculated arrogance.

"Can chance be left to chance in the New Order?" Heinz muttered to Helmut Pfeiffer, a fellow from the upper seniors with whom he sometimes played handball. Helmut had also been chosen for the outing although his hatred for Rüger was well known.

"Order excludes chance, of course," answered Helmut.

"What is your meaning, Pfeiffer?" Rüger was suddenly looming over him, red in the face.

"A witticism, Herr Rüger. A mere play on words," said Helmut.

"I do not find him witty," Rüger challenged, addressing himself to Heinz.

"Naturally you would not, Herr Untersturmführer," replied Heinz tranquilly. For his effrontery he received a sharp blow on the ear, and before he recovered his balance Rüger was in his place at the head of the group dismissing them. They joined their voices in the "*Horst Wessel*" song:

"Raise high the flags! Stand rank on rank together.
"Storm troopers march with steady, quiet tread . . ."

Rüger saluted them formally. "Heil Hitler!" they replied ritually.

The session was over and members of the team chosen for the expedition received mimeographed information leaflets explaining the effects of low temperature on bodily functions, the value of physical hardship in the acquisition of moral strength, and the mystical significance of discipline in the cosmic vision of the Führer. It was written in the same high-flown prose of Rüger's address and ended with a quotation from Hitler: "Instinct and will are what we need!"

When they were alone around a turn in the corridor, Helmut read out a sentence which was a syntactical horror, and Heinz came to attention and saluted: "A witticism, Herr Untersturmführer." They doubled over in laughter.

"Look out unless you want to get your other ear boxed," warned a comradely Oswald Müller, a senior already drafted into the Army, but permitted to wait for his final exams before joining his unit. "D.R., Dietrich Rüger, or Drittes Reich as we call Herr Rüger, is a vicious fellow."

"I do not find him witty," mimicked Helmut.

"He probably has plans to freeze our wits off," Heinz offered, but Rüger was now in sight behind them, and the boys quickened their step and headed toward the dormitory in silence.

The day of the outing was cold and sunny, with an icy wind whipping down from the snow-covered mountains. Each of the eleven boys was issued an extra woolen undershirt that reached to the knees, a knapsack packed with soldiers' emergency rations, snowshoes, and a small tin of Nivea cream to fortify the face against wind and frost. As the boys were preparing their gear, the headmaster suddenly appeared at the door. They stiffened to attention and answered his booming "Heil Hitler" with a chorus of stalwart "Heil!"s. Harimann's eyes were puffy and his heartiness forced as he gave them a synopsis of the leaflet they had received the previous day. Rüger stood listening with an expression of controlled contempt. In response the older man's hands fluttered and his voice faded until he could scarcely be heard. Sweat stood on his forehead. Finally he left, as though defeated and routed by Rüger's relentless stare.

The boys were then assigned buddies, and Heinz, the odd man, fell to Rüger's lot. A feeling of desolation gripped him as he returned the Untersturmführer's clap on the shoulder. "Buddies," said Dietrich Rüger, with a sardonic smile.

"Yes, *Mein . . . Führer,*" replied Heinz, matter-of-factly.

The line of bundled-up boys trudged over the snow-covered fields toward the slopes of the wooded mountains. They sang as they marched:

"*Auf der Heide blüht ein kleines Blümelein,*
und das heisst . . . Erika"

(On the heath blooms a small flower, which is called Erika [heather]) and their ardor rose to a pitch that was close to drunkenness. A single spirit seized the twelve and united them, barring private thoughts. The witchcraft worked by thin air, white light, pounding blood, and virile song filled Heinz with a dread as mighty as his comrades' soaring rapture. The morning seemed timeless; the sun perhaps stood still.

Heinz resolved to keep his concentration, as he had heard his father tell prisoners had done in the Great War, by the use of mathematical exercises. He counted in Polish by twos, threes, sevens, nines, all the while singing lustily. In a daring flight of rebelliousness, he began to recite the rosary to himself in Polish, an act of defiance that merited extremest punishment. It pleased him, and he shouted the Führer's praises, while deep within him marched the annunciatory greeting of the Angel Gabriel. "Heil Hitler," said his tongue; "Hail Mary, full of grace," prayed his secret heart. The discovery of this talent in himself stirred in him the desire for perfection as no other accomplishment or aspiration had ever done.

The fact that his mind was capable of this duality excited him beyond description, opened vistas he longed to explore. Like the revelation of sexual pleasure, this new knowledge held promise and mystery. Following the slow, shuffling path of the boys ahead, echoing their rhythmic chorus, Heinz concentrated on the crevasse between his two levels of consciousness, sounding it tentatively, to gauge his danger, like a child dropping stones down a quarry to hear the thrilling far-off crash.

Rüger instructed them to eat small portions of their rations hour by hour, so as to conserve energy and ward off fatigue and cold. He taught them how to rest without stopping their march, counting their breaths and shifting their weight from foot to foot as they climbed. He lectured them on mountains and glaciers and the dangers beneath the soft drifts. They crossed a broad snowfield and entered a higher snowfield pocked with bare stone ridges. Here they stopped and built a fire.

The boys hauled dead branches from among the trees and, as the fire blazed higher, Rüger grew excited and began to tear off the lower branches of fir trees to feed it. He swore strange oaths and screamed, "Make the flames higher. More wood!" They piled on more branches as he urged them on, and foretold in a high-pitched voice the destruction of cities in the great holocaust of conquest. "Warsaw in flames! Cracow in flames! Fire exploding into fire, a flaming torch. Bombs raining down fire, bursting red and black, the whole sky blazing." He laughed and threw his arms over his head, like the Führer opening a great rally. The fire glowed on his face and sparkled in his eyes. He seemed seized by a foreign spirit and shaken by its power.

"Everyone shout together—'fire!'" he commanded, and when they obeyed, he laughed triumphantly and shouted again and again, "Fire! Fire! Fire! Fire! Fire! Burn Warsaw! Burn Cracow! Burn Lwow!"

He heaped on green branches until a dense black smoke fouled the sky and began to damp the flames. The boys began to cough and to draw back.

"Infants. Babies. A little smoke, and they are defeated," Rüger taunted. A look of hatred was in his eyes as the fire sputtered in spite of his efforts to rally it. Finally he gave up and sank down in a crouch, depleted. In a tired voice, as though waking from sleep, he instructed them in taking quick naps to restore their strength on long winter treks. Obediently, they crouched down beside the stone ridges. Winded and bemused, they looked at each other blandly, like animals in a corral. A drowsiness dragged at their limbs and weighted their eyelids. Leaning against the sheltering rocks, they catnapped, trying to train themselves to rest and to wake up at a predetermined moment. The cold faded, as bone-weary fatigue blocked it out.

Heinz dropped into a deep sleep; his last thought was that he might freeze to death and never wake, but he felt no more fear at the idea than at a pleasant, whimsical fancy, a storybook death, white with snow and angels' wings. When he woke, he was cold and stiff. He opened his eyes, but he could see nothing. An eerie whiteness engulfed him; he thought he might be blind.

"Helmut! Oswald! Herr Rüger!" he shouted. Confused voices answered him from far away. He could soon make out the embers of the fire and the black shapes of nearby rocks, but beyond them a milky haze made the landscape invisible. The place where he had planted his snowshoes was behind one of the rocks, he could not tell which one in the confusion of shapes. He shouted again for the others, but could not tell from which direction their voices answered. He was suspended from sight and sound, but instead of fear, he realized, he felt an uncanny sense of triumph. If they were invisible to him, then he, too, was hidden, cut off from their world, immured where no enemy could harm him, no spy betray him, no bully torment him. The hazy brightness, opaque and protective, seemed a blessing.

He sat down against a rock. Even the cold seemed to buoy him up, and he let his mind drift on an inward-flowing current, toward a forbidden place: his native village, Polansk, that September 1, 1939, the day of his "execution."

II

4 P.M., *September 1, 1939*

Backed up against the wall of the central nave of the church of St. Stanislaw Kostka under the guard of two green-uniformed soldiers, neither one much older than himself, Heinz had felt the stone wall press against his spine. Then his name was Adam Leski.

Beside him the peasant Bialy shifted his spine to relieve the cramp under his shoulder blade, and the oiled steel O of the rifle's mouth directed at him twitched in response.

Bialy moaned, a frail, keening lament. The guard's boot scraped on the flagstones, and a metallic whisper chilled the vaulted nave. Bialy began to whimper and blew his wet nose on his sleeve. He was an old man—no one knew exactly how old—but he was still strong. He could load a cart with fifty-kilo sacks of potatoes and only last spring he had retrieved Adam's father's calf that was half sunk in the bog. But now, after hours of standing against the stones, facing the 98K muzzle and by the round, unmoving eyes of the soldier, with the scorching afternoon air turning his throat to dust, Adam saw the tough old man's strength fail and flicker out.

"Mother of God," Bialy whined. "Holy Mother of God, Queen of Poland." The stones behind him boring into his back, he reached out to catch hold of Adam beside him. The hand was cold, the palm damp. A harsh breathing came from the boy's chest and sweat ran down his face. When the guard struck Bialy, he loosened his hold on Adam, staggered forward, and slumped to the ground. Instinctively Adam moved forward to help the old man.

The guard stepped back and leveled the rifle at Adam, signaling him to get back in line and let the old man lie. A moan of surrender, almost of comfort, came from the heap of rags and bones crumpled at the boy's feet.

Adam tried to make out his father's expression. Boleslaw Leski was at the other end of the line. His eyes were fixed on the high window over the entrance at the church's west end, where the amber light of afternoon spoke of God's nearness. But Boleslaw Leski knew better; he had learned firsthand on the front of 1920 that God was not always at hand. He had a jagged scar down the middle of his face to prove it. He also had the evidence of nineteen years of blinding headaches and nightmares. Boleslaw Leski knew that God was a fraud—a secret he had kept from his only son, yielding to his wife's express wish. Beautiful Zosia, her thick blond hair falling to her waist when, at bedtime, she let him take out the combs and hairpins and spread it like a mantle over her back. Zosia's son was like her, soft and sensual, with a deep core of steel.

"O God," prayed Boleslaw Leski, "if You are not a fraud, let the boy live, for Zosia's sake."

"*Tot.*" The word came from outside in the street, distinct, a many-sided crystal cut from a deep mine and set up to shine in the abnormal emptiness of the village square. Even the peasants, who knew no German, understood. The word meant death.

"Untersturmführer Albrecht Milher."

"Yes. Dead."
"Died in the hospital."
"He never reached it."
"Dead on arrival."
"And the hostages?"
"What do you suppose?"
"Wait for your orders, Rottenführer."
"Orders. Yes, sir."

Leski wondered how many of the men had understood. But it was hardly necessary to understand the words: their meaning was clear from the excitement and fear in the faces of the soldiers. Leski knew Germans, and from the beginning had realized that whether the wounded officer lived or died, the hostages—he, Boleslaw Leski, and eleven others, including his only son, Adam—would be executed.

He wondered whether these new Germans, with their New Order, their new European and cosmic mission, their ruthless superiority, would afford hostages of war the dignity of a court-martial. As if in answer the German guard, unmoved by the old man's moans of protest and pain, kicked old Bialy, the carter lying on the cold flagstones. These men would not bother with formalities like a court-martial.

"Holy Mother of God," Bialy rasped. Adam Leski took an involuntary step toward the old man, and the second guard pushed him violently back against the wall.

"Halt!" he shouted. The vaulted nave took up the sound and the echo was a grim sentence of death. "No one moves."

Old Bialy lay still, his breathing loud and labored. The guard resumed his post. Leski did not want to look at his son, whose white shirt, blazing in the dusk of the old church, made him easy to spot just behind the collapsed form of the old man.

Somewhere down the line a man was singing softly, almost in a whisper, and the sound was like that of a song heard in sleep, or from across water in the quiet of night.

"*Boze cos Polske przez tak liczne wieki otaczal tarcza.*" (God who guarded Poland during so many centuries and protected . . .) The melody was reinforced by other voices, and a gentle chorus welled up to meet its echo, sliding back along the gold-flecked stone arches overhead. The two guards exchanged a look but said nothing. They held their rifles tensely, undeterred by the gentle communion of the men who were soon to die.

An officer entered the church and marched rapidly down the nave.

"Heil Hitler," he greeted the first guard formally, handing him a paper. The young soldier came to attention and returned the salute.

"The order of execution," he pronounced aloud, as though he had received a coveted gift.

"Heil Hitler," the second guard rejoined. The officer took back the paper and began to read: "In the name of the Führer, the victorious German Army, the glorious Reich . . ."

Adam braced his palms against the wall behind him. He looked at his father. The older man's face was still uptilted toward the high west window, but Adam saw that his eyes were closed. He had never known his father to pray, although he had heard him curse and blaspheme many times. "The Lord forgive you," his mother would chide, her eyes amused and her hands tender. He wondered whether now, at the frontier of death, his father was making peace with his Creator.

"All right! Move, there! March!" the officer shouted. The guard nudged Adam on the shoulder with his rifle butt, to push him into the line of men now moving out of the church.

"I am condemned to die," Adam clearly articulated to himself, unbelieving. "I am on my way to my execution. In the name of the Führer."

In his mind he could see the great darkened arena, the spotlights on the rostrum, the torches and banners, the sea of anxious faces waiting; the music, the excitement, the unbearable tension, the ecstasy as the great man strode forward, the hush as he raised his arm in salute, the roar of the litany, the frenzied worship. He knew the face and voice of the leader, this man for whose greater glory he was about to die. Newsreels, newspapers, radio broadcasts, posters had made the German Führer as familiar to him as any of the men he saw daily—the postman, his teachers at the

Gymnasium, the village priest. More real than his own grandfather, whom he had known in childhood, before old Leski fell off a ladder at the age of seventy and broke his neck. "Old fool!" his father had raged, not even trying to hide his tears. "Vain, pigheaded, goddamned fool!" he had mourned, pacing the house like a madman, pacing the station platform waiting for the bus to Katowice, cursing the beloved dead as though such ferocious grief must reach into the next world in the shape of a caress.

He himself would never mourn his own father, Adam thought to himself. Both of them would be dead before the sun went down on this warm September day. Dead. Adam could not really focus his mind on being dead. He stumbled across the square and waited to climb into the waiting truck with the others. He could see the asters and dahlias in full bloom in the tiny public park, fenced off from the formal walks he had crossed hundreds of times through mud, dust, snow, ice, water, autumn leaves. He felt numb; sounds and sights seemed far removed. Perhaps I am dead already, he mused. In the name of our glorious Führer, you, Adam Leski, are dead.

The men ahead of him in the single file were climbing into the truck; his father had already disappeared into its depths. Why does no one break out and scream that he refuses to die? he marveled. Why should twelve innocent men go so meekly to their graves? So silently? Why was there no one in the village to protest, to come to their rescue, at least to make some outcry—weep, wail, scream that God is mocked by swine, by German swine?

But there was no human sound, no sign of life. The village was as empty as a theater set waiting for the play to begin. The streets and houses looked like false façades made of painted canvas and held up by wooden struts. Adam pressed his fist against his mouth, but he screamed in spite of himself.

"Quiet!" A sharp blow over his ear punctuated the order. Blood trickled down the side of his head from the gash made by the rifle butt.

"I spit on your glorious Führer," he said under his breath. "I shit on . . ."

Behind them a single shot rang out. Although the day was

warm, Adam shivered with cold. Every man in the truck realized that old Bialy had been shot, lying as they had left him on the church floor. Terrorized, unmoving, defying repeated orders to stand, walk upright, acknowledge his death. In the dusk, Adam could see one or two of the peasants cross themselves surreptitiously.

The truck snorted and jerked forward. The driver was likely inexperienced or nervous, perhaps both. The two guards rode behind with the hostages; the corporal sat with the driver. The truck took the road to Piekary, which would pass the post office, the bridge, some ancient farm buildings huddled in a hollow. Farther on, where the stream took a leap down the rocks was the mill, then the borders of the Leski farm where perhaps his mother . . . Adam prayed she did not know of the arrests. Oddly, it pained him more to think of her anguish if she knew of their death sentence before their execution than to have her learn of it later when he could no longer imagine her pain. She would be forced to think of him as someone whose life was over. Incongruously, he thought of the day last summer when he had gone up in the hayloft with Basia, the new servant girl at the storekeeper's house. She came from Biasowice and loved to tease the boys about their innocence of certain well-known mysteries. She took money from them and made them promise not to tell. That day he had earnestly hoped that his mother was not thinking about him while he was performing those curious rites, but if she must find out what he was about then, that she find out about it later, when it was safely over.

In the gloom of the truck, he could see his father's form, upright and stiff, the way he held himself when his migraines came on, as though his neck were made of glass. There was no reaching him then; the wall of pain was impenetrable, behind it was fury.

The truck was passing over Adoski bridge; he felt the sudden rise, the rumble and rattle of the planks, then the downward swoop. Adam remembered the pleasurable fright he felt passing over the bridge as a child when his mother took him in the carriage on rare trips to Lubliniec. He used to pretend he was afraid (sometimes he did not have to pretend) that an evil troll lived under the bridge, as he had heard in fairy tales. He doubted now, for the first time, that his mother was duped, but she would hug him tight and put her hand over his eyes to shield him from the horrid sight, all the while explaining that there were no such things as evil trolls outside of storybooks.

Later on, when Adam had become a teen-ager, he used to meet his sweetheart, Lilka, near this bridge. They used to sit during the summer evenings watching the river and speaking of love. Adam wondered if Lilka was still in Warsaw.

All at once the sound of distant gunfire, tentative at first, then rapid and sure, came from the direction of the Rajewski forest.

"Uhlans." The word was not so much said aloud as passed telepathically among them. "*Jeszcze Polska nie zginela.*"

"Poland shall not perish," cried a voice; the men recognized it, but the guards were slow to catch the culprit. One of them shot into the air over the men's heads. Solidarity warmed them even in the instant of fright. Every Pole in the truck intensely dreamed the same dream, so powerful that it must surely shake the two young soldiers whose dead bodies were the simultaneous and explicit vision of eleven men.

Rifle shot and machine-gun fire, fainter, then louder, came intermittently across the meadow. A mood of exultation rose in the dark of the truck, sharp, palpable; the guards redoubled their watchfulness, fingered their triggers, swallowing nervously. If the Polish uhlans arrived in force and took the village, the tables would be brutally turned; executioners and victims would change places. Adam noticed that the young guard nearest him was pale and sweat was rolling down from beneath his helmet. Remembering old Bialy's agony and death, he was unmoved by the German's visible dread. "*Niech zyja Ulani!*" (Long live the uhlans!) he shouted, and then fell unconscious from a blow in the stomach.

When Adam regained consciousness he was being carried down from the truck by Wojtek, the local miller. They were in a field, he knew, not far from the ford where the cattle crossed to reach the pastures on the Rajewski side. Birch and ash and oak and pine mingled on the forest's edge behind them; willows and poplars outlined the stream's uncertain course through the meadow and back toward the mill, the bridge, the village, and, farther on, through Lubliniec until it joined the Warta River. Landscapes soon to be lost to him forever, he thought, a backdrop against which he would never play out his destiny.

"The uhlans?" he whispered to Wojtek, his head still spinning.

"Silence!" the guards ordered.

"Tanks. German tanks," Wojtek informed him recklessly. "The uhlans . . ." He made a gesture of annihilation. "Wiped out. Finished."

"*Ruhe!*" (Silence!)

There was no more to be said. Adam now took in the meaning of the village's uncanny silence during the whole of the afternoon. The villagers were all there in the field, pale, cowed, standing huddled in terror under the guard of many more German soldiers, exactly like the two who had been with the hostages since noon. Were they, too, condemned to die in the name of the glorious Führer, to avenge the death of one of his officers, whom he did not even know existed? Then Adam remembered tales and rumors: the villagers were there to witness the execution. It was to be a lesson, a warning not to shoot German officers, a nightmare to hound them sleeping and waking until the day they died.

"God grant Zosia is not there," prayed Boleslaw Leski, the unbeliever, now immured by pain. The gold-white brilliance that now enveloped him was his wedding day, gray and rainy from early morning, but now encapsulated in unearthly light that lifted his weight off the earth. The peasants believed it brought happiness to be married in the rain. Zosia had complained that her feet were wet and she would catch cold. She wore white slippers that came all the way from Warsaw. He loved her immoderately and could not believe his luck when she accepted him from among a flock of suitors. He was much older than she, and scarred, and known to be moody and unsociable. His great happiness had all but blotted out the tragedy that had ended his childhood—his mother brought home dead from a carriage accident when he was ten. They had tried to prevent him from seeing her body, but he had caught a glimpse of her strangely black face.

The guards shoved him brutally forward; a wave of pain engulfed him and the landscape darkened and blacked out; he groped for something to hold on to and, finding nothing, stumbled on in darkness. He thought of the night he was wounded. It was clear and cold; every sound was detached from its source, reduced to its essence by the dry mountain air. The front had moved back that day under heavy fire; his turn to stand guard had come after midnight. A burst of artillery fire from a near rise of ground that he thought was still held by Polish cavalry woke the men; then before he could give the alarm a shellburst felled him, left him blind and deaf. He woke in a field hospital, and his war was over.

Boleslaw Leski marveled to discover that in the hour of death the future is devoid of substance, whereas the past takes on depth and hue. Surrounding him, pale and numb, were other landowners—men he had lived beside, contended or connived with for gain or power, betrayed or been betrayed by; tradesmen and villagers he knew by heart—these men were vivid in his mind, their lives were interwoven with his own. Adam was in his heart a bright-haired baby running after his nurse, hiding in the maid's skirts, following his mother through the summer fields, bending beside her in the dappled light under the trees. A winsome schoolboy, now moody and violent like his father, now steadfast like his mother. Leski could not in imagination reach the youth whose life, shimmering on the edge of the present, was over at sixteen. It should have made him sad, but the rush of recollected images crowded out feeling. His world was ending and all his being strained toward clarity.

"You, there," a rough hand pushed him. He could no longer see. The piercing pain of his headache had blinded him as it often did during the recurring attacks. His hearing was by contrast more acute. He heard the Germans behind him quarreling in muffled voices.

"There are children there," said the voice of an older man. It was the gruff, proletarian voice of a career soldier, probably an old-timer.

"What do you care? Boys or men. Twelve hostages were our orders. They are all Poles. Scum of the earth."

"Slavs will be exterminated like vermin. Young and old alike. Why do you want to quibble?"

"Those two are under age. Schoolboys."

"The Führer's intention is to crush Poland, exterminate the Poles, wipe out the Slavs. What does age matter? Are you completely ignorant? Don't you know what we are doing here?"

"But those two are just kids. It isn't right." The voice of another generation, another world.

"Shut up, old man, or I'll turn in a report on you."

"The Gestapo will teach you the difference between boys and men.

"Yes, Herr Untersturmführer. Heil Hitler," said the old man. The New Order triumphed.

Adam heard his fate sealed; his two summers' tutoring stood him in good stead. He remembered his mother's insistence that he improve his German, and the sprightly, graying priest who came twice a week in the long vacation to improve it. They read Goethe and discussed philosophy. He even did geometry and algebra in German, although Father Sebastian was bored by figures and preferred to talk of politics or religion or a man's duty and calling in life. Adam had wondered what his duty and calling would be. Father Sebastian wished it might be Holy Orders, but Adam saw himself in the handsome uniform of the Polish uhlans, joining his regiment in some far city, invited to great houses, dancing with perfumed, bejeweled ladies before going to meet danger and adventure. Now he saw that his duty was to die.

A tremor shook him and fear shattered him like a strong wind. He could not stand firm; his knees shook, his hands trembled, a kind of bleating sound was rising unbidden from his breast. The men around him closed ranks; a strong hand touched his shoulder in brotherhood. It was the village buffoon, a man seldom seen sober, a trapper and a poacher not noted for honest dealing. "Poland shall not perish," he mumbled. "Holy Mother of God.

Pray. *Ora pro nobis.*" In his extremity his mind stumbled down the well-known mazes of drunkenness. Adam stopped shaking and bowed his head. He held himself stiffly, not to show less courage than a wretched sodden half-wit like Janek who knew how to die.

Adam decided to look once more at the village, the trees, the people, to say good-bye to all he loved. The gloom of the frightened faces of the villagers expressed the tragedy of the situation. They contrasted with the beautiful landscape lighted by the last sun of this day.

As the soldiers made ready to raise their rifles, a car appeared with four men in the black uniforms of the Gestapo. The officer in charge of the execution saluted, raising his arm straight and shouting "Heil Hitler!" The Gestapo man next to the chauffeur, a stocky, squarish man with short gray hair and a scar on his face, returned the salute and spoke for a few minutes with the commanding officer. Another hope? Could there be a change of orders? The prisoners stood silent, hopeful.

The four Gestapo men left the car and stood facing the prisoners, ready for the spectacle of the execution.

A faint wail came from the huddle of villagers. It reached a wild crescendo as the corporal gave the order and a blast of rifle fire felled the eleven men.

Adam awakened in the cellar of a monastery. The first thing he noticed in the meager candlelight was a crack in the ceiling, and after that the face of his teacher, Father Sebastian, his tutor. He was sitting there watching Adam. Father Sebastian smiled, seeing Adam alive. A few hours later a doctor arrived and extracted the bullets lodged in Adam's shoulder and chest, operating in the darkness of the cellar. Shaking with fear for his own safety, the doctor did as best he could. Afterward the Sisters of Charity, who had been living in the monastery, kept him hidden until he recovered.

Meanwhile Father Sebastian went to Katowice, got in touch with Adam's aunt, his mother's sister, who was married to a German lawyer named Oscar Weiss. They provided Adam with the papers of a boy named Heinz Hauptmann, a German who had been killed along with his parents in the first days of the war. After their deaths Weiss had taken the papers from the wreckage of his neighbor's home for use, should such a situation arise.

Adam spent a month with his aunt and uncle, hiding in a storage room. In the meantime, Weiss contacted Hauptmann's bank, arranged a guardianship, and got Adam admitted to a school in the Alps, run by an old classmate.

This same Adam Leski was now surrounded by a white haze that seemed to seal him off from the hurt of his memories of the hostages' deaths and of the terrifying dawn when he had been dragged from the grave.

The wind, carrying particles of ice, blew in his face. The other day, when he and the other sixteen of his classmates had sworn to give their lives to the Führer, began to haunt him. Huddling in the snow, facing the blast of the wind from the mountains, he felt the events of that day rasping in his mind, counterpointing his horrifying memories. The words of the oath claimed his upper consciousness. Over and over they went, like a broken record that could not be stopped.

"I swear to devote all my energies and my strength to Adolf Hitler. And to give up my life. So help me God."

"In the name of the Führer, I sentence you."

"Before this blood banner I swear."

"Ready. Aim. Fire!"

"The name of the Führer. Condemned to die." The refrain would not be stopped, but rushed on inexorably, while the white mist held him in thrall and the voices of the others died out in the distance.

"The Führer is condemned to die. I swear to devote all my energies. I am ready to give up my life that the Führer may die." A smile was on his lips and drowsiness was claiming him. "So help me God," he murmured aloud. "I am ready." The words released him from the spell, as though he had found the key that unlocked the puzzle, and he drifted off again, unafraid. The frozen fog stood guard around him like a band of angels. When he woke, it was gone, and the winter sunset was red on the western peaks. He found his snowshoes where he had left them in the snow, ate the last of his rations, and started off in the direction of the forest. Following the downward slope, he was sure to come out in view of the Oberschule, although by that time it would be night.

III

February 1940

Heinz was in the school infirmary, suffering from exposure and frostbite. He had reached the school gates after midnight, having spent useless hours following the lights of a power station, where there was not even a guard to take him in. He collapsed in the lodge of Franz, the gamekeeper, where Franz's wife, Maria, put him to bed on a cot while her husband went for the housemaster. Telephone lines were down because of the blizzard that had caught Heinz within sight of the school. "An hour longer out in that weather," remarked Maria, "and the boy would be dead instead of almost dead." She fussed over him, rubbed his feet, poured brandy down his throat.

Neufeind, called out of a sound sleep, was furious. He was required to report any serious illness to the boy's parents, and in this case it was more complicated, because the boy was an orphan, and his guardian, as far as anyone knew, was a bank. The school might be judged remiss, and people of influence might raise questions. The history of the Oberschule would not bear close scrutiny in certain quarters.

Neufeind determined to get the truth out of Rüger although the task was distasteful to him. He distrusted the young gymnastics instructor and also was somewhat intimidated by him. Rüger had the air of an informer, and Neufeind felt instinctively that it was a wise policy to stay in the young man's good graces. On the other hand, if Rüger's conduct of the outing were to be censured, it might put a dent in his arrogance. And, all things considered, it would be better for everyone if a Gestapo informer were guilty of a student's accident than if the blame fell on the school. Neufeind had no heart for a battle with Rüger but he would risk it if he had no choice.

He decided to go first to the infirmary to inquire after young Hauptmann's health before making any move. The boy was delirious, talking in Polish, calling for his father and a father named Sebastian, reported Kotecha, the aged nurse. Kotecha knew a smattering of several Slavonic languages, having served in the Austrian Army in the last war and spent part of it in Siberia escaping from prisoner-of-war camps with raggle-taggle bands of Poles and Cossacks.

Heinz could not keep even a swallow of water down, though he kept complaining of thirst.

Against the grayish sheets, the boy looked flushed and overwrought; he stared intensely at Herr Neufeind and then said clearly, "No, that is not the one." Then he closed his eyes and seemed to doze off. Beads of perspiration rolled off his face and darkened the pillowcase.

"How bad is he?" Neufeind inquired.

The old man shrugged and pulled up a chart from an envelope taped to the foot of the bed.

Neufeind glanced at it and put it back, irritated.

"In your professional opinion, Herr Kotecha?" he asked sarcastically.

"He is not in danger," the nurse replied glumly. "But he is very sick."

"How long, then? I mean, will he miss school? A month? Less?" There was a regulation that a report must be made if a student missed more than two weeks.

"Two weeks, not more," Kotecha obliged. "If the lungs hold."

"I see," said Neufeind. "I shall speak to Dr. Harimann. I want you to keep a careful record."

"Yes, Herr Professor," the old nurse answered, somewhat mollified.

"I will make a special lavender brew," he added.

"See that I am informed immediately if he takes a turn for the worse."

"The doctor has not come yet, Herr Professor. I sent the porter for him early this morning. The telephone is out," Kotecha told him.

"Well, we must be patient. You've done all you can," said Neufeind, more kindly. He had eased his own apprehension, and furthermore he knew he might find in Kotecha an ally useful in the confrontation with Rüger, if it came to that.

Although visiting Harimann in his office without first making an appointment was frowned on, if not actually forbidden, Neufeind went directly to the headmaster's office. He found Harimann pacing the room excitedly, a sheaf of blueprints unfurled across his desk. He was talking to himself and occasionally slapping the papers triumphantly as he paused to peer down at them myopically.

"Norbert!" he greeted Neufeind warmly. "Come here and look at this!"

"Herr Direktor," Neufeind hesitated. The mood was one he knew well. Until it passed, there was no remedy but to humor him. Clearly Harimann's recourse to his "tonic" was becoming more and more frequent, his elation higher and the subsequent depression and apathy more erosive. His lined face and yellow-gray skin made him look ill and old, although he was probably not yet fifty.

"Look at this, my good man. I've had plans made for the new school. Here we'll have the soccer fields, here an archery range, here a rifle range . . . stables for horses. Look at these blueprints for an underground shelter! Ten meters down, a regular bunker for the whole school. Separate quarters for the staff, steam heating, kitchen, telephone cable—we could operate down here for months. Then we'll have a tower, overlooking the whole Salzkammergut. We'll see the Rabenberg peak in fine weather. All in neoclassic style, something grand, impressive. I tell you, Neufeind, this school will be the envy of every academy in Süddeutschland and Ostmark. In the entire Reich." He paused and clutched the edge of the desk, as though to anchor himself.

"Very interesting, Herr Direktor. Remarkable. Extraordinary," Neufeind murmured.

"Money will be no object," Harimann raved on. "We'll open a fund-raising drive. We'll rename the school Heinrich Himmler School. Money will pour in. I have great plans. It only takes imagination, will and imagination."

"Extraordinary, Herr Direktor," Neufeind rejoined, abandoning hope of bringing up the problem of a student who might not live.

A bell rang and Neufeind took the opportunity to escape. As he excused himself, he said uncertainly, "I must talk to you about the Hauptmann boy, Herr Harimann, when you have a moment. We have an unfortunate incident on our hands."

"Ah, yes. Young Hauptmann. Come back after assembly, Neufeind, and I'll show you the maintenance shed. A beauty."

As he spoke, Harimann's pupils were dark specks of anthracite, shining and darting from one object to another. His agitated gestures punctuated thoughts he could not express. Neufeind closed the door with a sigh of relief. He wondered how long it would be before Harimann's madness became intractable. He usually timed his injections so that he did not confront colleagues or students until he had leveled off after the initial elation. Neufeind realized he had made an error in going to the headmaster's office without an appointment; he would doubtless have to pay for it in the coin of petty humiliations.

Neufeind took his place in the procession to the assembly hall, a Baroque chapel left over from the centuries when the school was a monastery and, later, a Catholic boarding school. Only the chapel recalled its past. Now it was used for the various rites that had replaced the worship of God—patriotic rallies, observances of national holidays, school ceremonies and assemblies. Today the student body had been called together for a routine lecture on safety and the measures to be taken in case of bombing or other catastrophes of war. A plan for the defense of the school by upperclassmen and staff was to be outlined. Neufeind mused upon the unlikeliness of an assault by either prostrate Poland or the apathetic Allies on a strategically useless spot like the Oberschule, known chiefly for the beauty of its mountain scenery and the bracing effect of its air. Perhaps if the grandiose visions of the headmaster were to materialize—the tower with its view of Salzburg castle and the well-appointed bunker—the danger of attack would increase. He looked about to see whether Harimann had attended the convocation, but did not see him.

Before the lecture was over, Rüger left the hall hurriedly. Following him with his eyes, Neufeind glimpsed the white-coated form of Nurse Kotecha in the vestibule. Perhaps events were taking their course without his intervention.

After the assembly was dismissed, Neufeind made an exploratory detour past the headmaster's office, but his door was closed. Loud and agitated voices reached him; Rüger, Kotecha, and the school secretary, Fräulein Rahmann, were in conference with Harimann. The subject could only be the Hauptmann boy's misadventure. Through the window Neufeind caught sight of Franz, the gatekeeper, scurrying up the path—summoned, perhaps, to give evidence against Rüger.

"The boy's family will have to be informed," Harimann's voice vibrated histrionically. The tone was unmistakable—in that exhilarated state he was not easily outflanked. Possibly as a junior instructor Rüger did not know Harimann's history, but the school secretary certainly did. She was devoted to Harimann, however, and would not remind him in front of the others.

After teaching his senior math class, Neufeind wandered purposelessly about, trying to decide whether to seek out Rüger and question him, return to the headmaster's office, or pay another visit to the infirmary. He decided to go talk to Dr. Harimann, but he ended up at the infirmary. As he took hold of the door handle, Rüger rushed out, nearly knocking him down.

"What news?" he inquired civilly, fencing before any match was declared.

Without any apology, Rüger looked at him coldly, as though to say, "Ask for yourself if you want to know," but visibly thought better of it. He might need allies. He shook his head. "Not good. The doctor's come and gone. Kid's got pneumonia. Fever of a hundred and four. Delirious. Confounded ass. All his own fault. And now I've got to make a report to send home. All for an idiotic foul-up. Am I supposed to let ten boys freeze while I go looking for one? Why couldn't he stick with the group like the rest? In that white-out no one could tell what was going on. Every man for himself. That's what they're supposed to be learning, for devil's sake. So now I suppose I'll be transferred to taking the fifth graders on maneuvers around the soccer field. Damn thick-headed Polak." Rüger was white with rage and frustration.

Perhaps more was at stake than his status in the Hitler Youth, Neufeind reflected.

"Get a grip on yourself," he said kindly. "The boy's going to pull through. Tough as they come, that kid."

"Harimann's got it in for me. He hates my guts."

The older man put his hand on Rüger's shoulder in a fatherly gesture. Although he did not like Rüger, he sensed the young instructor's misery. He was also grateful that Harimann had taken care of the interrogation that he himself had been dreading. And Rüger had evidently come off poorly.

"Guess I'll have a talk with Kotecha. You can safely put off writing your report for a day or two. There won't be any mail going out until they get the roads cleared of branches and the wires fixed. Bad news usually can wait. It won't spoil."

"Right," said Rüger, somewhat cheered. "You're right. Much obliged." He saluted, and Neufeind gestured vaguely, pushing open the infirmary door. Kotecha was sponging the boy with alcohol to bring the fever down. He sat propped up against the pillows, gasping for each breath.

"Look at these scars," Kotecha said in a conspiratorial whisper.

"I wonder about them. Some kind of operation?" The boy's body was marked with incisions, one on the left arm, two on the shoulder. They were recent wounds, not completely healed. Neufeind had seen them often, and assumed the boy had been wounded in the bombardment in which his parents had been killed. Yet on close inspection, he noticed they looked more like bullet wounds. Perhaps he had tangled with Polish partisans before he was rescued. The story was muddled in Neufeind's mind, if indeed he had ever known it.

"Whoever sewed him up, it must have been a horse doctor. Look at that," Kotecha remarked, pointing to an ugly pouch of flesh.

"Umm," replied Neufeind. "How's the fever? Any improvement?" He thought it politic not to venture an opinion about the scars. He remembered that the boy was personally recommended to Dr. Harimann, and his acceptance at the school had been somewhat hasty.

"Dr. Warnis is another horse doctor. Dunderheaded old fool. I can guarantee you the kid will pull through." He pursed his lips to mimic the doctor's northern accent. "I give him a slim chance. Very slim, Herr Direktor. The prognosis is poor. Doesn't know his elbow from . . . We'll see him in his grave before this Heinzel here." He fondled the boy's head and pulled the shirt tenderly down over his scarred body.

"Why didn't you tell Rüger that, then?" he said.

"Untersturmführer Rüger's peace of mind is no concern of mine. I only repeated what the doctor said," Kotecha replied. "He needs to have someone put the fear of God into him. My guess is he let the kid get lost on purpose to scare him. I'd lay money on it. That's the kind of mean bastard he is. Of course he didn't arrange the blizzard, and now he's scared himself. I hope the family raises hell."

Neufeind suddenly decided to confide in old Kotecha. They were united in their suspicion and dread of Rüger, after all. "They boy is an orphan," he said. "He has no family, only a guardian. An old acquaintance of Herr Harimann's, I believe. It is not generally known, however."

"I see, Herr Professor," Kotecha replied in a voice that promised discretion. "Bad luck." He seemed genuinely moved at this news, then suddenly his eyes clouded. "You know what they do in case an orphan dies in the school, God forbid?" Against all the rules, the old man crossed himself.

"What do they do?" Neufeind asked. It was a question that as far as he knew had never come up. He hoped in passing, as he noted Kotecha absent-mindedly caressing the boy's hand in sympathy, that he had not given Heinz too assiduous a protector.

"They call on the *Gauleiter* to stand as godparent and give him a nice burial. Do the honors, so to speak. It happened in the school I worked at before."

Dietrich Rüger wouldn't relish that bit of news, thought Neufeind to himself, but aloud he said heartily, "But this is all nonsense. The boy is going to pull through." He picked up the chart, on which the fever held at 104 degrees. He gave an audible sigh.

"Dr. Warnis sent a special emergency requisition for sulfa. It is a miraculous drug. As soon as the roads are cleared we'll have it. Then you'll see a change."

"Good, good," Neufeind said doubtfully, taking his leave. "Say a prayer for him, then," he needled Kotecha, who shot him a frightened look.

"Heil Hitler, Herr Professor," he saluted feebly. The old man's hands were trembling, Neufeind noted. He did not mind playing on the childish fears of a simple-minded creature like Kotecha; it was just idle sport and meant no harm.

Heinz lay in a white haze, which swirled around him like the blizzard. His bed seemed to rock up and down like a boat in rough waters. When he penetrated the fog, he saw faces; one face remained, while others came and went. The one that stayed, hovering over the foot of the bed, never changed his expression, and never spoke. It was a man he vaguely knew and inexplicably feared. The man stared at him unmoved, menacing in his stillness. Voices came to him clearly, but the words did not make any sense.

He dozed off and dreamed of lying buried in the ground. He was unable to move and struggled mightily against his own paralysis. A heavy weight pinned down his legs, but unless he moved, he knew he would suffocate. Trying to heave his body sideways, he felt a sharp pain pierce his shoulder. He rose to another level of consciousness, in which he knew he was in bed and not under ground. The bullet wound was real, but it had healed. He remembered the pain of lying in a cellar surrounded by nuns. A doctor probed the bullet wounds, poured on alcohol or some similar liquid fire; he had gritted his teeth to keep from screaming. When he saw the scalpel, he had given up and screamed. Then he fainted. Father Sebastian had held him down; Father Sebastian was weary, yes, because he had carried him all that way. Memory swirled around him, and he moaned, trying to piece together events he could scarcely distinguish from his fevered dreams. Father Sebastian had pulled him up out of the grave and carried him in the dark. He had pleaded with the nuns to take him in, and they, not wanting to violate the cloister by letting a strange boy in, had finally consented to make him a cot in the cellar. The doctor had closed the incision with clamps, and remembering, Heinz woke up fully, with a scream in his throat. He opened his eyes, and the unmoving face became clear to him. It was a portrait of the Führer, the great leader of the Reich to whom he owed his death. To whom he had pledged his life in a solemn oath. There was surely a way out of this puzzle, if only his fevered brain could find it.

The following morning, Heinz woke with a clear head. His fever was down, and the gentle rocking of his bed had ceased. The portrait of Hitler on the wall opposite his bed receded to its proper distance. It was a blurred and slightly yellowed print, not particularly sinister, and Heinz inspected it calmly. He remembered his father's death, in the days of forbidden memory, when he was Adam Leski, a boy with dreams of growing up to be a uhlan and fighting for Poland and the Blessed Virgin. He remembered the legends of his childhood, of sons avenging the deaths of their fathers, sometimes aided by a magic talisman or by supernatural beings, sometimes by their own wit and courage, sometimes through the intervention of the Queen of Heaven, who loved them for their purity and valor. There was one picture he remembered of a youth kneeling before the altar during his vigil on the eve of his knighthood; it showed him kissing the hem of the Virgin's gown as she materialized above him in a shaft of unearthly light. Heinz smiled at his own boyhood dreams, as though he were an aged sage and the boy Adam Leski his own romantic grandson. Now he saw clearly the harsh substance of his oath of knighthood. It was a sentence of execution.

IV

March 1940

The rain was falling hard. There was nothing unusual about rain this night in early March 1940. Rain fell often at this time of year in this area of the Alps not far from Berchtesgaden. The two men walking on the narrow mountain path were well prepared for the rain. They wore rubber raincoats and heavy shoes. They were alone on the path but nonetheless spoke in whispers.

The older of the two, Harimann, spoke: "On July 27 I handed over the papers to Michael Komm, who was supposed to bring them to Oscar Weiss. As you know, it was not possible to continue our foreign contacts from here; Weiss, who lives in Katowice, was supposed to carry on from there."

The men were walking now on a steep passage, and the younger, a man in his mid-forties, stopped to catch his breath. He was not used to outdoor exercise and the effort tired him.

The thick lenses of his glasses were of little help in the darkness. His narrow face, with a small mustache, was wet from the rain and this disturbed his sense of orderliness. He wiped his face frequently with a neatly folded handkerchief. The two moved on.

"Weiss was unable to accept the papers since he was under surveillance by Polish intelligence," Harimann continued. "Weiss told Komm to get in touch with his brother-in-law, Boleslaw Leski, a Pole from Polansk, a village about eighteen kilometers from the former Polish border."

"I know the rest of the story," the younger man said, stopping again to wipe his thick lenses. "Our military intelligence reported the contact of Komm with Leski. The matter reached Malec of the MACABR unit. He quickly arrested Komm, who then committed suicide." The younger man spoke quickly. "I know Malec well. I wish he worked for us. He is very methodical, a typical policeman, a good detective. Great in detail!"

Harimann wanted to mention something but it was impossible now to interrupt his superior.

"We have to find those papers but do nothing to arouse Malec's suspicion. I can't reassign him to another task. He is now in the Amt 1, in charge of the protection of the Führer's life."

He cleared his throat, and Harimann took advantage of this interruption to interject, "Good fortune and luck help sometimes."

The two men were standing now on the top of a hill and the rain began to come down harder. "Immediately after the beginning of the hostilities, Malec and his group crossed the border and were searching for these papers," Harimann said. "Fortunately for us and unfortunately for Malec, the key witnesses were executed as hostages; those were the Pole, Boleslaw Leski, and his son, Adam Leski. Malec held Frau Leski in custody for a month in Breslau, trying to extract the information, but he couldn't make her talk. I doubt very much that she knew where the papers were hidden and even if she had known, she would not have revealed this information. She might have assumed that the papers had some value for the Poles. Anyway, she is now dead. She died during the interrogation.

"They searched vainly for the papers," said Harimann. "They

took the house apart. There was nothing. They dug the garden several meters around the house: still nothing. The papers must be hidden kilometers away, and . . ."

The younger man interrupted: "Too bad about Komm. He might have been successful in the Munich assassination." Georg Elser had failed Bürgerbräukeller, maybe Komm would have succeeded."

The two men turned around and started to walk back down the hill. They walked in silence, each engaged in his own thoughts. When they approached a clearing they stopped.

"There will be other opportunities. Where others have failed, some day an assassin will succeed. You must look for the right man," the younger man spoke.

Harimann took off his glove and shook the wet gloved hand of the younger man. "Good luck."

The younger man walked away. Harimann stood in the darkness. After a few minutes he heard the clicking of boots and a distant voice shouted, "*Jawohl,* Herr Reichsführer!" Then he heard the noise of a starting car engine. The car drove away. Otto Harimann walked down the hill whistling, confident that Heinrich Himmler was the man of the future for Nazi Germany. Only Adolf Hitler stood in his way.

Two weeks later, Harimann was standing with two men in the lounge of the Hotel Imperial in Vienna. The elegant hotel was crowded with bejeweled ladies dressed in the latest fashion, uniformed officers, and well-dressed civilians. No one in this gathering seemed concerned about the war. Laughter rose gaily from the tables in the grandiose lobby. No one paid much attention to Harimann and his companions. A man with a graying crew cut wearing a plaid jacket shook hands with Harimann, who spoke in German.

A big fat man in an expensive serge suit, white stiff collar, and a silver-gray tie approached Harimann's companion and translated into English, "Sir, for your achievement you deserve a guerdon."

"I do not understand. What do I deserve?" said the man with the crew cut.

"The highest reward," the fat man repeated, adjusting his monocle. "I hope you shall have a most delightful journey to New York."

Soon the man with the crew cut left. The fat man sat down with a sigh and ordered a glass of Kirsch. "You know, Herr Piersohn," Harimann said, "you have just translated the most important exchange of words anyone has ever been privileged to interpret."

Piersohn, still exhausted from the task, waved his hand and with pleasure caressed his gray mustache.

Otto lowered his voice. "You see, Professor, the future is ours. That's true. Elser failed but we will succeed one day."

"I know you will, Herr Harimann," the professor said.

"I am glad you have learned to trust me," Harimann said.

The professor wiped his forehead with a silk handkerchief which sent the aroma of hyacinth across the table. "I am glad you have recruited Neufeind. You learned well the rules of our game. You are intelligent, Herr Piersohn."

"Neufeind will be good for our purpose," Piersohn said, after ordering another Kirsch. "He is an excellent marksman. One day he will fear for his life because of his Jewish background. He will be good, better than Elser."

"I am not sure about it," Harimann observed. "Fear is important—to achieve a certain loyalty from your collaborator. Just as in your case. I recruited you before your certain confinement in one of our concentration camps and possible death for your affairs with little boys, I know I can rely on you to some extent." He paused. "I do not think you would be capable of killing, would you?"

Piersohn hated to be reminded of the unpleasant incident and of Harimann's miraculous intervention. "I guess not," Piersohn replied. "Not yet. Why can we not live without killing?"

"My dear Herr Piersohn, killing is what this war is about. I personally have contributed a lot by laying plans for the elimination of Jews, Gypsies, Slavs, and other undesirable peoples. We must clean Europe, the world." Harimann became excited. "Killing a few people is easy; killing millions requires an organization and a method. My ideas are enthusiastically received both by Himmler and Hitler."

"So why bother with plans regarding the last named!" Piersohn whispered.

"There is a great deal of difference, my dear Herr Piersohn. One day you will understand." Harimann adjusted his horn-rimmed glasses. He wanted to say something more but a group of officers was passing by the table. When they were far enough not to hear, Harimann went on, "One day you will find out. There are too many people, too many undesirable races in this world. Did you read the works of Madison Grant?" Without waiting for an answer he continued, "The world must belong to the Nordic race. I have made plans to take away children in Poland who are Nordic and rear them in Germany. This way they will swell the ranks of the Nordic race."

"But we are still fighting England," Piersohn observed. "It is populated by Nordics."

"That's what some of us don't like," Harimann said. "We are wasting our U-boats. We should make peace with England."

Harimann looked around, but they were sitting far enough away from other people not to be heard. Nevertheless he lowered his voice to a whisper.

"England would not negotiate with Hitler. They would with Himmler."

"How about France?" Piersohn asked.

"It will be a blitz. Like in Poland we will finish the French in a matter of weeks. One day when we have achieved peace with our race brother, the English, we can take Russia. Plenty of good land . . . and inferior races. You do understand me, Herr Piersohn?"

"In the meantime we must wait, Herr Harimann. It is difficult for me to obtain my favorite cigars."

"Not for long. I don't mean your cigars, but the takeover of France."

"How about Russia . . . ?"

"You will have to wait a little longer, Herr Piersohn. A little more preparation, and the peace treaty with England."

"But little Finland is doing so well against the Soviets. We should be able . . ."

"That's a Russian trick," Harimann said. "They want us to believe that they are weak so that we can feel free to throw all our forces against the English without fear. In reality the Soviets are much stronger than they appear or pretend to be . . ."

At this moment the waiter in tails approached discreetly: "There is a telephone call for you, Herr Harimann."

When Harimann returned he sat in silence for a few minutes before speaking. "There will be a fight soon; we will win that struggle. You see, I just learned that our enemies are alert. Malec suspects me. Rüger, Malec's spy, made some new reports on me. Fortunately, he did not find anything."

V

April 1940

When he returned to the dormitory, Heinz was thin and wasted. He spent long hours sitting on his bed staring at his hands or looking out the window. "It is the new drugs," Herr Neufeind explained to anyone who cared to listen. His studies were not affected, however. He easily made up the work he had missed in math, chemistry, and physics; the Rassenkunde teacher let him off with a recommendation to read a tedious book by Hans Günther; and he did passing work in German and Latin, no better or worse than he had before. He conscientiously joined in early morning calisthenics, although by doctor's orders he was allowed a period of grace before resuming the daily workout in the cold air. Waiting for his bread and ersatz coffee, he would hide his hands under the table so the others would not see how badly he was shaking. He ate ravenously and was always hungry —which was not very different from the other boys who had never been sick.

When he could, Kotecha surreptitiously fed him extra rations, hidden behind a screen in the infirmary, under the pretext of having to check his blood pressure or give him an injection. Slowly his strength returned, but the damage to his spirits was not mended. Nightmares haunted him day and night.

One day as he passed the gatekeeper's cottage, he saw a group of agitated boys out back of the shed, crowding and craning their necks. He joined them to see what was the center of attention. It was a wounded dog, inert and covered with blood, probably shot by hunters, explained the gatekeeper, and left for dead in the forest. It had dragged itself as far as the clearing, where he had found it and brought it home. It was unlikely to live, and Franz proposed to put an end to its suffering with a clean shot in the head. The boys were told to clear out and let him get on with it.

Some were only too glad to be excused from witnessing the killing; others were morbidly fascinated and begged to be allowed to stay. Heinz had no desire to see the shooting, but found himself rooted to the spot. His feet would not move, and a strange lassitude possessed him, passing over him in waves. Franz shrugged and ordered the few remaining spectators to stand back out of harm's way. He took an old rifle from the shed and fired it at the dog's skull, all in one unbroken movement. A harsh gasp, like paper tearing, escaped Heinz's throat, and he doubled over and fell to the ground. His body stiffened in a convulsive seizure, he gasped for breath, then as suddenly went limp and began to moan and come to himself. The dog all but forgotten, the boys looked on horrified, waiting for Franz to give some directive.

"We had a maid once, used to have the fits," offered Karl, a fat boy of about ten. "It's nothing."

"Shut up, smart ass," advised another.

"It's the drugs. He's been in the hospital," an older boy said to Franz. "Herr Neufeind says it's because of the drugs he's a bit . . ." He traced a quick spiral at his temple.

"Loony," interpreted Willi, louder than necessary.

"Get out now. All of you. Quick," Franz ordered. "I'll take care of him." Heinz had got to his feet unaided and, though somewhat wobbly, couldn't quite understand what the fuss was all about.

"Did I faint?" he asked Franz, bewildered. "What happened? I feel strange." Then he remembered the dog, and his eyes traveled to an inert mound covered with a burlap sack. Sobs shook him, and he buried his face in his hands. Franz led him into the house, where he finally managed to say, "Poor dog." Then, as if in explanation, "I had a dog when . . ."

"That's all right," said Franz. "Your dog's all right."

"Yes," said Heinz and stared at the floor lifelessly. After a while, Franz gently led him out the door and he trudged up the path to the school. He put his hands over his ears, remembering the shot. It was the first he had heard since facing the German firing squad, in another life. He did not want to see the others or answer their questions, so instead of going to the study hour in the large hall, he went to the library.

There a bronze bust of the Führer was displayed on a pedestal, while modest niches around the walls held plaster likenesses of Frederick the Great in uniform, Goethe with a laurel crown, Schiller, and Beethoven. A few boys were browsing about the shelves or working at the tables, surrounded by open books. Heinz took a seat where he could stare into the Führer's eyes, lifeless shadows in metal, but death-dealing. It was said that the Führer knew no fear; in the Great War he had braved enemy fire to carry messages to the front. He knew that no bullet would kill him; he had faith in his destiny. And, indeed, no bullet had stopped him from carrying out his mission to be the savior of the German people.

Suddenly Heinz's face lit up and in his excitement he nearly cried out. The Führer's bullets had not killed Adam Leski either; his destiny had yet to be fulfilled. He went to the shelf and selected a book at random, so that his excitement would not attract attention. He sat turning the pages, his blood pounding in his ears. The book was a history of medieval warfare, with line drawings of fortifications and armor and weapons. A sketch of archers caught his eye, assault units of crossbowmen and longbowmen. He remembered his father's precious crossbow, an intricate contraption like a musical instrument. He used to travel all over the countryside to compete with other crossbow clubs in knocking a wooden popinjay from a pole. Boleslaw Leski was known as a keen sportsman and crack archer. He hunted deer with the crossbow, too, on occasion. The sound and kick of a rifle set off his headaches, so he had perfected the art of killing with a weapon that hums and whispers. Heinz let himself be transported into a past he had been warned to forget. His father's rough wool trousers tucked into the tops of his boots, the ritual oiling and polishing of the stock, the strong squarish hands moving nimbly, caressing the smooth wood.

His father had promised to teach him to use the crossbow when he could hold it securely and notch the string. But the summer he was fourteen, and strong enough to force the prod to bend, his father had suddenly become busy with meetings and trips into town and mysterious errands around the villages and farms. And the next year Adam had started spending his time in the village with friends, loafing in the square, talking about girls and great deeds, and going to the city to study, and joining the uhlans. At home he had spent his time with Father Sebastian, at his lessons, or walking in the woods. He saw little of his father, and the crossbow was idle in its case under a bench in the study. Heinz sighed. It was a sport for men who had leisure, in times when the long days between planting and harvest stretched out like the dusty roads linking village to village, unchanging, inviting the imagination to follow a tranquil bent. Men who had no ambitions, nor rancors, no compelling needs beyond the care of their land. That was the life Adam Leski was to have inherited, before the jackbooted killers marched into his village and devastated his past and destroyed his future.

He stared at the bronze bust in its place of honor. A gleam of recognition nagged at him. He had seen that man in the flesh. Not the Führer himself, but another. Clean-shaven. That was the clue. The sculpture, lighted by the overhead bulbs, emphasized the facial structure—the long chin and undistinguished brow—rather than the characteristic mustache and lock of hair. Heinz could not place it, but the question would not leave him. He tried to summon up past images, but failed. Then the final bell rang. Study hour was over, and the boys trooped to their dormitories to prepare for bed. The senior boy on duty in the library put out the light and waited by the door for the stragglers to leave. As he passed the bust of Hitler, Heinz made a boy's gesture of contempt with his fingers under the cover of darkness.

The next day was April 20, the Führer's birthday. Classes were suspended, and the boys were to march into Nyphelheim—wearing their Hitler Youth uniforms. The Gauleiter was to make a speech, and the Führer's greetings to the nation would be broadcast from loudspeakers in the marketplace, where the troops of boys and girls from the schools and the labor and farm units in the district would stand in formation to listen and cheer.

After breakfast there was an inspection of boys' quarters—beds, shelves, footlockers, uniforms. After the parades and speeches, who knew what officials of the Party might take it into their heads to visit the Oberschule? There were to be games and track competitions and at night a great bonfire in the field beyond the gate. Local or visiting SS, Gestapo, or Army officers might decide to join in the festivities, so the headmaster had sent out a special directive that the whole school must be impeccable.

Rüger was the inspector for the east wing, where Heinz was quartered; he marched into the room in a foul mood, cursing and rasping out orders. Heinz turned red as he approached (each boy stood at attention beside his bed) and suddenly began to hiccough loudly. A giggle swept through the long room, and Rüger turned around in fury. He said nothing. Heinz hiccoughed again, uncontrollably, and a chorus of laughter answered him. Rüger took hold of Heinz's bedding and yanked it off the bed; he overturned his footlocker, spilling out books and underclothes. A bag of marbles loosened its contents over the aisle and the tiny balls scurried over the floor in disarray. The laughter mounted to a hysterical pitch and boys doubled over holding their sides with merriment.

"You are all confined to grounds on Sundays for a month," shouted Rüger. "Pick up that crap, Hauptmann, and make your bed properly for a change. Line up in five minutes in the courtyard." He marched out of the room, omitting to inspect a half-dozen beds. Boys scuttled under the beds in search of marbles; most were returned to the chamois bag, and Heinz's friends helped make the bed and put the footlocker in order.

Their mood of comradeship and hilarity lasted all morning as they lined up, sang the ritual songs, and saluted in unison the day God put the infant Adolf Hitler on earth for the salvation of Germany. They formed into squadrons and marched into town. People in passing cars and trucks shouted greetings or blew their horns saluting the handsome spectacle of hale, pink-faced youth. They paused now and then to change flag bearers and catch their breath. Heinz could see that Rüger's surly mood had not changed. Marching beside his squadron of younger boys, Rüger felt his demotion rankle. Since the mountain expedition and his subsequent change of command in the Hitler Youth, he had held a black grudge against Heinz, whose nervous fear of him only made him more angry.

As the column neared the outskirts of the town, it rounded a bend where a small, ancient stone church stood close to the road, boarded up now and used only by occasional tramps or lovers. Weeds grew between the trampled dust of the roadside and the flagstones of the narrow porch. As the boys marched smartly toward the tower at the entrance to the main street, with its great gilded clock and graceful arch, their step quickened. Flags could be glimpsed through the arch, and crowds milled about the arcaded street in holiday clothes. Every eye but one was trained on the arch, that window into the town. Only Heinz noticed a man standing in the shadow of the little church's porch. To stop or turn his head would be breaking formation, but his eye caught the image of a gray-haired priest standing back out of the sunlight, scanning the squadrons of boys as they passed. He recognized the man. It was Father Sebastian. The piercing blue eyes, stooped shoulders, crooked bony hands clasped and unclasped in nervous agitation. By the time he had confirmed the priest's identity, he was past the arch and the color and movement of the street almost blotted out the shadowy impression.

The morning passed like a dream. He followed his comrades from place to place, responding to orders automatically, as though under a spell, trying to recall the image of the priest. Had there really been a man there? Had he seen him clearly or only dreamed him? Was it possible that the likeness was so close? Could it be a different man, a double? Could it conceivably be Father Sebastian? Was he there to look for Adam Leski, a boy he had pulled out of a grave in a Polish village and carried to safety? He surely knew where Heinz was, because he had arranged for his uncle to fetch him from the convent and would have learned how he came by his German identity, his German parents, and their money left in trust for his schooling. Father Sebastian would know, but why should he want to follow him there and risk exposing his masquerade?

Heinz was so agitated that he was hardly aware of the broadcast of the Führer's speech. Listening to the crowds hail Hitler with frenzied welcome. Listening to him announce the forthcoming German victory, and a thousand years of peace, greatness, world dominion. Images of the leader came to him as he listened: the yellowed print in the infirmary, the portraits in every classroom, in shopwindows, flanked by flags. The bust in the library. Another image flashed over these familiar pictures. Flashed and vanished. It was clean-shaven, and now it had a visored casque. A soldier. Germany was full of them, but that one had a peculiar face and a meaning for him—or for Adam Leski. He dropped the pursuit of the soldier's image, since like a faint star, it disappeared from sight. When he trained his eye full on it, he tried instead to summon up the figure in the dim porch of the church. Beset by ghosts, he looked around him at the black and red banners, the uniformed children and young people, the black-garbed SS troops, and saw them all as figures of his dreams. He had a clear vision of interchangeable worlds.

The boys' marching line was to re-form at the town gate, after an interval of free time in which they could stroll around the town and satisfy their appetites with buns and pastries. Heinz went straight past the point of the rendezvous, heading toward the abandoned church a few hundred yards down the road. He found nothing there to confirm or refute his impression of the morning. Some poorly dressed children were throwing pebbles into a puddle by the steps. He asked them if they had seen the priest, and the oldest scoffed.

"There is no priest." He gestured grandly toward the boarded-up door, implying that Heinz must be a bit slow-witted.

Heinz thanked him coldly and began to walk back toward the arch. A stone stung him between the shoulder blades, and giggles followed as he hastened his step without turning. A volley of pebbles fell short of their mark just as he rounded the turn into the gate. Hatred and anger surged in him, but he knew he must not draw attention to himself. Or to his question about a priest, supposing he had really seen one, and supposing that this one was Father Sebastian. It was better to endure the mockery of a few peasant brats. He reflected that village children in Poland would not be so cruel to a stranger; they would keep silent or run and hide, out of shyness, if an older boy in a school uniform addressed them. But the children of a superior race threw stones at a stranger's back.

He stood dejected in the archway waiting for the others, since the great clock told him they would soon appear. Opposite him was a small iron door that led to the tower's staircase, he supposed. A single strand of cobwebs floated free from its handle, catching the light. As he stared, wondering at the foolhardiness of insects who spin in such precarious spots as doorjambs, the door opened and a black-robed figure stepped out. Heinz caught his balance by clutching the rough stones of the archway. Father Sebastian crossed the street and smiled at him benignly, as at a stranger.

"Do you wish to go to confession, my son?" he asked in a low voice, not turning his head to left or right.

"Yes, Father," said Heinz, scarcely above a whisper.

"I will be in St. Gertrude's on Sunday afternoon. You may come to me there," said Father Sebastian. Nodding politely, he made his way down the crowded street and disappeared.

Dietrich Rüger was suddenly standing in the place the priest had left, sneering at Heinz as though he had caught him in an infraction of the rules.

"What did that old bugger want?" he asked menacingly.

"To know the way to the public urinal," Heinz answered tranquilly. He took strength from his own duplicity.

Rüger did not look very satisfied, but could find no reason to believe Heinz was mocking him. "Well, keep clear of that vermin," Rüger advised him. "They are all spies and perverts." He stalked off without waiting for an answer.

Heinz felt strangely elated at the thought of his coming rendezvous. He remembered that Rüger had ordered the whole senior dorm confined to quarters on Sunday, and the thought of defying or eluding him only heightened his sense of adventure. He would tell his friends he was meeting a girl, and they would be sure to regard him enviously, supposing he was meeting one of the shop girls with large breasts. He was pleased with himself the rest of the day, even though his team lost at soccer, and Rüger, their coach, was in a rage.

That night he dreamed a man with a bronze bust in place of his head was driving a car, pursuing him through unknown streets. He woke up screaming to find Herr Neufeind beside his bed shaking him awake. He was drenched in sweat. In the dream his legs were paralyzed and he could not run from the monster in the car. Now he kicked his feet free in relief and sat up. "A nightmare, Herr Professor. I had a terrible dream."

"It is the drugs, poor lad," said Neufeind kindly. "It will pass."

"Yes, sir," said Heinz. He did not want to lie down for fear he would find himself back in the nightmare street, facing a horror that was not even death but something unnamable. He now realized it was the bust of the Führer in the library that had haunted his dream, the unsolved puzzle of the resemblance trying to break through to consciousness. A soldier in a car. There were thousands of them on the roads. It was not much of a clue.

"Try to sleep," advised the drowsy housemaster.

"Yes, sir," said Heinz, reluctantly lying down. He resolved to stay awake until dawn.

Neufeind went back to his room shaking his head and mumbling to himself. The war. The drugs. Without father or mother. Wounded in the bombardment. Caught in the blizzard. Soon to be drafted into the Army. No wonder the boy had nightmares.

He soothed himself to sleep with an outpouring of pity for Heinz's misfortunes, eased by the generosity of his own warm heart.

The next Sunday the senior boys' penance was lifted by order of the headmaster himself. He had received compliments in writing from the local authorities, commending the behavior and turnout of his students on the Führer's birthday, and in an expansive mood of good will, sustained by an injection of his tonic, he had reversed Rüger's peevish order.

Heinz made his way to the town, had a bun at the bakery with his friends, and went by back streets, inquiring the way to St. Gertrude's. It was a modest church in a poor section near the old, crumbling town walls. He chose a side entrance that stood open and, genuflecting nervously, began to explore the side chapels, since there was no priest in the central nave or at the main altar. In a small chapel toward the rear, a gray-haired priest knelt in contemplation of a faded painting representing the martyrdom of St. Stanislaus, whose head was split open by the arrogant King Boleslaw's sword. Heinz knelt beside him and directed his eyes toward the painting. He waited for the priest to speak.

"You did well to come," said Father Sebastian, addressing him in Polish. "Were you followed?"

"No, Father," said Heinz. "I came by the back streets."

"Good," said Father Sebastian. "Now listen carefully, and if I get up and leave, stay here awhile, then go home quietly. I will be back next Sunday. Do you understand?"

"Yes, Father . . . and I am so happy to see you again." Father Sebastian remained silent, until finally he spoke:

"I prayed again, thanking God for your miraculous survival."

Father Sebastian rose and sat down on the bench. Heinz joined him.

"As long as I live, my son, I will never forget that late afternoon in Polansk. I happened to be in Lubliniec on the first of September, bringing the last sacraments to Countess Podolska, who has been dying for the past five years and receives extreme unction as others do Holy Communion. I returned by the forest path, since the roads were suddenly overrun by the enemy.

There was fighting in the woods but I could not tell where. Toward evening I was approaching the main road from Polansk when I came upon a clearing where you, your father, and the other hostages were to be executed."

Father Sebastian searched for a handkerchief, then wiped tears from his eyes.

"I heard the blast of rifles fire . . ." Father Sebastian continued. "The Germans pushed the bodies into the ditch. . . . A Polish-speaking soldier gave the order to fill the grave although the field was growing too dark to see clearly. The Germans then marched the people back to the village."

It was quiet in the church and Heinz lowered his head. He wondered whether his mother had seen the execution.

"I remained to pray for the dead," Father Sebastian said. "I do not know how much time passed before I heard your moaning. I groped about and found you. I got you out of the grave and covered the other bodies carefully . . . out of holy respect and also because I did not want the Germans to count them the next morning. I cannot say how, but God gave me the strength to carry you to Bylice . . . two kilometers."

Father Sebastian stopped and looked at Heinz.

"I hope, my son, that you can devote your life, saved by a miracle, to a great cause."

Heinz nodded assent. His eyes did not leave the holy picture over the altar.

"Did your father hide any papers before he was arrested?" Father Sebastian asked. "Or give them to anyone to keep?"

"I think so," Heinz answered, caught off his guard. "I helped him bury an iron box. He didn't say what was in it. I thought it was money or jewels."

"Did your mother know about the box?"

"Yes, Father. I'm sure she did."

"The papers must be very important to the Germans." Father Sebastian wiped his nose with a white handkerchief. "An SS unit came to Polansk . . . high-ranking officers . . . a Hauptsturmführer Malec, his first name Rudolf . . . the Obersturmführer Friedrich Cart. They must belong to a special unit. Possibly Amt

1, responsible for Hitler's safety." Father Sebastian spoke as if he were carrying on the conversation with himself. "They could not . . . no . . . they would not come to investigate some Polish matter. It is a puzzle. Your father could never have been connected with the Underground. I have known him for too many years." Then, turning to Heinz:

"You didn't see the stranger who delivered the papers?"

"No, father, I did not. I told you . . ."

"I am glad. I am glad, too, you are far away. Is your money coming regularly? The bank is supposed to be sending it, the Dresdener bank."

"Yes, Father."

"You have recovered very well. When I picked up the wounded, I prayed for you but . . . I doubted whether you would make it. It is God's will." Father Sebastian made the sign of the cross over Heinz's head. "It was lucky for you that your mother's sister married Oscar Weiss, a good German. It was his idea to place you here. In the lion's den . . . it is safer. How are you making out here?"

"I manage. It is . . ." Heinz wanted to tell Father Sebastian how difficult it was for him but decided not to add to the many problems Father Sebastian had to face.

An old woman knelt at the altar rail and began to tell her rosary, whispering loudly. Father Sebastian rose unhurriedly.

"God bless you, my son," he said in German and left the chapel. Heinz remained, as he had been instructed, although he longed to run headlong after his old tutor. It would be a week before he could hope to hear the answers to the hundred questions that hummed in his brain. A week to wait and hide his anxiety. He looked long at the picture of the martyred Bishop of Cracow, who had defied the tyranny of the brutal king. He scarcely took in the bloody scene as he recalled the words that had just passed between him and Father Sebastian, trying to fathom their meaning. He remembered clearly the night his father woke him and showed him the spot at the edge of the beet field where he had buried a small metal chest in the earth, admonishing him to remember it, but never to reveal it to anyone until the Germans were driven out of Poland. Adam Leski had promised, and the two of them had filled the hole and tamped down the earth. His mother had met them at the door, and sent him to bed without a word. As he rounded a bend in the stair, he saw her embracing his father in the dim hallway.

Now the old woman had finished her prayers and was bundling herself to leave. She bowed to the floor before the altar as he had seen peasant women do in Poland. Homesickness pierced him like a chill. Then he rose and left the church by the front door with a crowd of children. Making his way back through the side streets to the center of town, he tried to suppress his impulse to look into every shadow for a glimpse of a black cassock, which reason told him would not be there.

VI

May 1940

The week was a long-drawn-out lesson in patience. Heinz went out of his way to talk with Heinrich Stroebe, a German boy brought up in Poland, like the dead Heinz Hauptmann whose name and inheritance were now his. It was a relief to be able to speak Polish, to sing snatches of old hit tunes, to reminisce about his boyhood vacations in Zakopane. Heinrich was not the kind of boy he would have chosen for a friend—he was sullen and loutish and liked bullying the younger boys and making senseless demands on the help. But he was a link with home, and Heinz was willing to tolerate his faults for the link with the past the association would afford him.

When Sunday came, he found his way to the chapel dedicated to St. Stanislaus. Father Sebastian was not there, and for a moment Heinz's heart sank for fear he would not come. He knelt at the altar rail and contemplated the bishop in his martyrdom. A man soon joined him, but from the corner of his eye he could see that it was a stranger in a brown tweed suit. He did not turn his head, out of an instinct for concealment, although there was nothing to prevent a schoolboy visiting a church. When the man said in Polish, "I'm glad you have come, Adam," Heinz looked at him in amazement. It was Father Sebastian. "Shall we go for a stroll where we won't be interrupted?" Father Sebastian continued smoothly. "I'll explain about these clothes in a moment." They went out of the church and entered an ancient graveyard beside it.

"I am here illegally, you understand," Father Sebastian said reassuringly. "I won't be recognized wearing trousers. Strange how an ordinary suit can be a disguise, isn't it?" He laughed. "Luckily."

"Yes, Father," said Heinz uncertainly. "What am I to call you?"

"How about '*Wój*'—'Uncle'? Uncle Sebastian. That's quite simple, eh?"

"Yes. Uncle," said Heinz. "I'm so glad to see you," he added impulsively. They walked among the tombs, now and then pausing to read an inscription or admire a carved relief.

"Why did you want to know about the box?" Heinz began. "Has it been dug up? Did the Germans find it?"

"No. No one knows where it is hidden. Now that your mother is dead." Father Sebastian seemed to hesitate.

"But my mother was killed long ago. The same day my father was. You told me so yourself."

Father Sebastian was silent.

"Do you mean she wasn't shot by the Germans? You told me the Gestapo went to the house. She threatened to shoot and they killed her."

"No, Adam. She was taken away to be interrogated. About the box, I believe. But she is dead now, God rest her soul. It was necessary for you to believe she was dead so that you would save yourself. No one could have saved her. I could not even find out where she was."

Heinz was pale and shaky, but he held back his tears.

"But she is dead now," he repeated. "They interrogated her. But you said no one knows. She never told them. They tortured her until she died. But she never gave in." He remembered his father teasing her about her stubbornness. "Zosia should have been a man," he would say. "She would have made a general."

"She was a brave woman, Adam. You must not think of her sufferings but of her victory. . . . And then, son, another thing." Father Sebastian paused. Heinz noticed how tired he looked. His hair, which had been brown when Adam had known him as a teacher of German in Poland, was now gray.

"I discovered that the third man, the SS man investigating the papers, is Dietrich Rüger."

"But he is here."

"This is what puzzles me most. First I thought that he was here to spy on you, but that doesn't make sense."

"He could be. He hates me."

"No, definitely not." Father Sebastian looked around. "He began his assignment here early in November while you were still recovering, still with the nuns. At that time we did not know where you would be living. Even your uncle assumed you were dead." Father Sebastian took a few steps as if intending to leave the cemetery. Then he stopped. "The four of them belong to the most vicious SS unit. It's called MACABR. The name comes from the first two letters of the two superior officers, MALec and CArt, and the first letter of the other two. One of them is Rüger; the other's name I don't know." Father Sebastian paused and looked at the mountains in the direction of Berchtesgaden, only some twenty kilometers away. "There are rumors that another faction of the Nazi Party, the Himmler faction, is after the throne, the power." Then he looked at Heinz. "I suspect that is what the MACABR unit is investigating."

He shook his head. "Cart was the one responsible for the death of your mother. She was a brave woman. You can be proud of her."

"Yes, Father," said Heinz. He felt numb; anger, cold as ice, was taking possession of him.

"I came to caution you about the papers. They are still hidden, and you are the only one who knows where. The Gestapo want that box very much."

"I understand, Uncle Sebastian," said Heinz. "I will be careful."

"The best way to be careful is never to go back to Poland, where someone might know you. The people of Polansk were dispersed, and much of the village destroyed. You might run into someone from there in any part of Poland. If someone ever discovers that you are hiding as Heinz Hauptmann and the Germans learn about it, they would torture you to find the papers. The Germans don't like to be reminded of a mistake they made."

Father Sebastian looked around. "Now listen to me carefully. I am going away. If we meet again, you must not speak to me. Even if I speak first, you must not show that you recognize me. I cannot say any more than that. Try not to tell that I was here, unless you have to."

"Yes, Father," said Heinz. "I'll never tell."

"Good-bye now. God bless you, my son." Father Sebastian made the sign of the cross, and then strode quickly to the gate and held it open for Heinz. "Good-bye, nephew," he said in German.

"Good-bye, Uncle," Heinz replied. He watched as Father Sebastian walked rapidly down the street and turned off into a lane. Then he wandered around the town trying to think about what he had learned. Until he could control his rage, he could not trust himself to act rationally.

He would not think of his mother in prison, subjected to God knew what horrors, until she died of them. He thought of her as she was that last summer, busy with the house, the garden, her dogs, the servants, visits to friends, a new dress she bought in Warsaw and then didn't like and took apart and fussed over until it suited her. She had the kitchen full of preserves when the fruit was ripe, first cherries, then gooseberries and black currants and rose petals, then his favorite, crab apples. Janka, the little round-faced maid, would grumble at the extra work; then his mother would send her home for a day with a basket of jams and fresh cheeses for her brothers and sisters, and she would be ecstatic. Later on there were rabbit pâtés to be made from a French recipe or quail to be put up. Sometimes Janka's little sister Marysia came to help, but the child was all thumbs and not very clean. Adam loved to be in the kitchen when the women were working. His mother would make him tea and give him herbs to chop or berries to sort. Her thick blond hair tied up in a blue scarf and her face intent over the steaming pots, she looked more beautiful to him than when she was dressed up and ready to go to mass or into town to shop or make visits. He remembered how she looked coming to fetch him from his piano lessons after an afternoon in town—small and neat and elegant, with white gloves and a black hat setting off her bright hair, its dotted veil falling down over her nose. He was proud to be seen with her in the streets, where people would turn to watch her go by.

His friend Lilka had once confided that she longed to look like Adam's mother when she grew up, and he took it as a compliment to himself. Lilka's own mother, Adam's piano teacher, was not a beautiful woman, but she had a queenly bearing and an innate elegance that Adam had no name for. She was from Warsaw and had finished the conservatory, and could have had a career as a concert pianist, since her family was unfathomably rich. But she fell in love with a medical student and threw all her family's dreams out the window to elope with him. His family had been just as chagrined at the match as hers, since they objected to her being Jewish, but the couple had lived happily and Lilka and her brother Wacek were the most indulged children in the grammar school. The girls all envied Lilka's clothes, which came from Warsaw's smartest shops, and the boys coveted Wacek's expensive English Rover bicycle, his radio that could tune in all the capitals of Europe, his Schlesinger tennis racket.

At one time Adam had been in love with Lilka, and dreamed of rescuing her from burning buildings or runaway horses. He had given her a bracelet with a tiny pearl in it, bought with a lavish gift of money from his godfather, and she had secretly kissed him on the lips after his lesson, while their mothers were talking in the next room. He had somehow been made aware that he could not marry Lilka (they were eleven or twelve at the time) because she was half Jewish. But romantic stories of her parents' elopement fed his fantasies. When he had saved her life at the risk of his own—in these heroic scenes he was always a uhlan officer in full-dress uniform—her parents would plead with his to let the young lovers marry and everyone would agree that it was God's will.

The last year before the war, Lilka had gone to Warsaw to attend a stylish finishing school and study music with her mother's old teacher, and he had not seen much of her, even on holidays. Now he was supposed to believe that she and her elegant mother were hopelessly flawed, inferior beings, while crude oafs like Rüger and pitiful slobbering old fools like Harimann were destined to rule over them like gods. And over him, too, and all his kind. They were authorized to take his mother to prison and put her through unspeakable tortures until they killed her.

The lights were fading, and Heinz realized he had been walking aimlessly about the town for several hours. He took the road back to school, and passed the little church by the archway. By the time he reached the gatehouse, his grief and fury were buried so deep they were part of his bones.

For the rest of the term Heinz often thought of his mother's death. In his mind he saw his mother beaten by uniformed Gestapo henchmen. He imagined others whipping her, still others inserting needles under her fingernails. In his dreams Heinz saw his mother hungry, kneeling, while the Gestapo men kicked her with their boots, in front of the large portrait of Adolf Hitler.

Heinz could not stand to see the smiling face of the Führer looking down on his mother's pain. In his mind he began to inflict upon the Führer's portrait the same tortures his mother had experienced. With time the portrait acquired the dimension of the man: Adolf Hitler.

And remembering how his mother had died as the result of such tortures, Heinz realized that Hitler, also, must die. He, Heinz Hauptmann, once Adam Leski, must kill him. Only the thought of the buried papers and his duties to his father made him hesitate. He knew that he could not expect to escape from such an adventure alive and yet he was the only one who knew where the box was buried. The Gestapo wanted that box very much, Father Sebastian had said. He wondered many times, as he tried to solve the puzzle, why Father Sebastian had not asked him exactly where the papers were buried.

The sin of despair often masquerades as something else, Father Sebastian had taught him. He had not understood at the time, but now thought he had a faint notion what the obscure teaching meant. Was his willingness to throw away his life in a desperate gesture a blind for the eclipse of hope? The meeting with Father Sebastian was a kind of watershed; his life from now on would take a new course, cut off from his childhood faith and from human love. He would sharpen himself into a deadly implement, and when the time came, he would strike with the force of despair.

As his resolve crystallized, it seemed that every victim of the German tyranny must have thought of it. The torturer of his mother, his father's murderers, the man who had sealed his own death sentence were one. He must kill the Führer. At first he was afraid to look his teachers and classmates in the eye for fear they could read his thought. He felt as though it were written across his brow. Then calm took over, and life seemed simple and full of ease. He began to study with zest and to excel on the soccer field. The day he arrived at his resolve, he walked out over the new spring grass, and almost without thinking stopped and picked a four-leaf clover. Another lay not far from it and seemed to detach itself from the green shapes around it and call to his eye. It was a curious challenge then to find them, not by searching, but by waiting for them to declare their symmetry to his receptive glance. He found four that morning and pressed them in his math book. Later he would mystify the younger boys by exhibiting this strange faculty. He was not sure himself where it came from.

One day he dropped in on Kotecha in the infirmary, where he was always sure of a welcome and possibly some sweets, and found the old man shuffling a deck of cards. "Playing solitaire?" he inquired.

"No," replied Kotecha. He put his fingers to his lips in a conspiratorial gesture. "I'm asking the tarot cards a question."

Heinz had to use the full power of his imagination to see him in the role of seer.

"Different people do it different ways," the old man shrugged. "Stars. Lines of your hand. I ask the cards. Do you want to know something?"

"How do you mean?"

"Just ask the cards a question, they'll tell you the answer."

"Is it a game?" asked Heinz.

"If you like. Yes," said Kotecha. "I get bored waiting for boys to cut their finger or get a bellyache. I play with the cards."

"What should I do, then?" said Heinz. "Ask them that."

Kotecha shuffled the deck and held it out to Heinz to cut. The boy took the strange card that turned up, stared at it, examining it from every side. "A four-leaf clover!" He opened his wallet and showed the old man a dried four-leaf clover. "It brings good luck."

"There is no clover on the card," said Kotecha, mystified.

"Inside the cup." Heinz pointed to a golden chalice with a four-petaled symbol floating on a red background inside its rim. The tiny figures had struck him among the other bright-colored images on the card, just as the rare four-leaf clovers seemed to stand out to his eye in the profusion of a clover bed.

"This card tells you that you are led by others, but that you act only for yourself. Your search is ended. Success is delayed if the card is upside down," Kotecha recited.

"Was it upside down?" Heinz asked.

"I can't remember—you picked it up and began looking for clovers," Kotecha reproached. "Now, don't tell a soul I have these cards. It is forbidden, and I will get in trouble."

"I won't tell, I promise," said Heinz solemnly. "Word of honor."

"Good boy. Now I have something for you—a piece of strudel my sister sent me as a present." The old man hid the cards and set out two pieces of cake on coffee saucers. They ate in silence,

Heinz making appreciative sounds. Hastily he ran the tap to rinse his plate and fork and stood up to go.

"Thank you, Herr Kotecha," he said. Then impulsively he opened his wallet and took out the four-leaf clover. "Keep this to bring you good luck." He raised his finger to his lips in imitation of the warning that Kotecha had given him. The old man winked, and Heinz went on his way.

VII

Summer 1940

As the term drew to a close, there were special assemblies to celebrate the advance of the German armies into Holland, Belgium, France. The boys, exhausted from studying, daily gymnastics, day-long military maneuvers, were exhilarated at the news from the front read in hysterical tones by an overwrought Dr. Harimann.

Heinz was invited to spend the first weeks of the summer with his classmate Andreas Wendel, who had been in the infirmary when Heinz was brought in delirious. Andreas had left before Heinz regained any clear notion of what was going on around him, but he had returned periodically to see how he was. Kotecha had no doubt passed on the information that Heinz had no family, and Andreas, being a kindhearted boy, had secured permission from home to bring a schoolmate back for the vacation.

Andreas was a reader of novels and poetry and somewhat anemic. He admired the grace and strength that made Heinz every captain's first choice when they made up teams for soccer or basketball. Also, his romantic nature made him curious about someone who had been wounded in the war and left alone in the world at sixteen. Heinz accepted the invitation gratefully as a welcome alternative to remaining at the school all summer. After Father Sebastian's warning he could not risk returning to Katowice.

Andreas was so overexcited by news of the fall of France that he ran a fever and had to stay in bed. He planned a writing career and would begin his apprenticeship, he thought, as a war correspondent. Though it was probable that his poor health would keep him out of the Army, he visualized himself as a soldier fighting for the Reich and keeping an exact journal of his experiences that would bring him fame after the victory. He confided these plans to Heinz.

Heinz reciprocated his friend's admiration, since he himself was poor in German and could not write a decent composition. Andreas and Heinz talked about Rabenden, where the Wendels now spent the summers; they used to vacation in the Obersalzburg, but their property had been sold to the government because it adjoined the Berghof estate, and the Führer did not want private cottages so near his country retreat.

Heinz was careful to show no special interest at hearing this news, reserving for the long summer ahead all the questions that crowded his mind. Here was a boy who had grown up on the land that was now part of the Führer's country seat. He would know every crag and ravine and forest trail, every waterfall and brook. If it had been the Leski property the Führer had acquired, Heinz reflected, he would be able to tell every detail of the terrain for miles around. There would be many days in which to find out whether Andreas could do the same.

The boys took the train on the day after their last exam and arrived in Rabenden that same evening. Three ladies got off at the same station and immediately began an animated conversation with Andreas' parents, who were waiting on the platform. They were summer residents like the Wendels and had a year's news to catch up in five minutes' time. When the garrulous trio finally scurried off to check their luggage, Andreas introduced Heinz to his mother and father. They seemed old enough to be his grandparents; Herr Wendel was a gigantic man with close-cropped gray hair. He held his head to one side, as though listening. Frau Wendel, who was short and stout, had bright brown eyes that had an anxious look, as if she were perpetually expecting bad news, but her manner was brisk and practical.

Andreas had been born when his mother was nearly forty, and both parents doted on him. They were genuinely glad to have someone his own age in the house to keep him occupied during the holidays, and Heinz's robust blond looks and deferential manners made a good impression on them from the start. He took in their kindhearted welcome with gratitude, suddenly aware of how much he had missed his parents and the shelter of family life.

Days began late in the old-fashioned summer cottage of the Wendels, with its low-ceilinged, shadowy rooms full of old photographs, souvenir china plates decorated with city escutcheons and famous landmarks, petit-point samplers, and woodland scenes painted on cross-sections of the trunks. The rooms were amiably cluttered with miscellaneous furniture banished from various city rooms. The boys would dawdle over breakfast and tease the little red-headed maid, then make their plans for the day in consultation with Andreas' parents. Often they took a picnic lunch and went for long walks in the mountains, and Heinz's excitement mounted as he gleaned details of the former Wendel property by deft questions and hints.

One day they took the train to Berchtesgaden and went for a day's excursion in the forest. Along the mountain trails they occasionally met armed guards patrolling at random. "It means the Führer is in residence," said Andreas knowingly. His family's former property lay within the great enclosure, somewhere between the two high fences that kept intruders off the sacred mountain. The house had been torn down and the outbuildings leveled; now forest paths, paved like city streets, crisscrossed the property. The boys drew near to the outer fence and peered through, and Andreas tried to locate familiar copses and clearings. The landscape had been changed, and his memories were foggy, but he was sure of the general location because of the giant firs and spruces that locked their branches overhead, casting the whole forest into perpetual twilight. The boys gathered the giant cones and threw them at the high branches to startle birds and squirrels. Then they tossed them over the edge of a gorge to hear them rattle on the stones far below.

They ate their picnic on a mossy knoll circled by great oaks, and afterward climbed into the lower branches and tried to peer into the forbidden enclosure, hoping to catch a glimpse of some high-placed guest on an afternoon stroll through the woods. But no one from the Berghof ventured beyond the inner fence. Only an occasional guard could be seen, or sometimes a large police dog, keeping the deserted buffer zone safe from intruders.

"I wonder if there are caves anywhere," Heinz speculated. In Poland he had once gone into a cave with his father, far under a mountain into the depths of the earth. He was about eight at the time, and was frightened by the total silence and darkness. His father carried a flashlight and tried to amuse him by deciphering the names and dates previous visitors had carved on the damp stone walls, mostly obliterated by the water endlessly dripping down the rock. He was still afraid of caves, yet fascinated by them; old tales of malevolent subterranean races haunted his childhood dreams.

"I know there is a cave," Andreas recalled. "We used to take our visitors there. My father would know exactly where. I'm not sure whether it would be inside the fence or not. We used to go by car when my father worked for the Krohler iron foundry. He had a company car, even on vacation. He was an important executive before he retired. That was why he had to join the Party, even though my mother was against it."

"Let's look for the cave! Try to remember what else was near it. Maybe a waterfall or a lookout point," said Heinz excitedly.

"I know. There was a shaky little bridge we'd cross, over a gorge," Andreas recalled. "And we'd watch the sun set behind the mountain just across, so it must have been on the eastern slope of a valley. But it would be far from here. We always went by car."

"We'll try to get a map and come back and search for it, shall we?" said Heinz. "Maybe your father would draw us a map. He will surely remember." He sat down against a fallen log and unwrapped a last slice of poppy-seed cake and broke it in two. Andreas sat down beside him and they watched a blue haze engulf the peaks as the late summer afternoon blended into evening. They drank warmish sweet tea from the same canteen, then prepared to go back to the station.

"After the war, I'll come back here and write my book," Andreas planned. "I'll build a little rustic hut and live alone. Will you visit me?"

"I'll come and bring you girls to distract you from your celibate life. Or maybe you'll already have a sweetheart hidden away in your forest retreat?" Heinz teased.

"After I publish my book, I'll be known. Then I'll marry. A serious girl, not the kind you're thinking of."

"I'm going to sleep with a hundred girls before I marry," said Heinz. "I think I'll start next term, or maybe this summer. How about bringing that round little Gretchen up in your attic room?" He enjoyed provoking his strait-laced companion.

"My mother will send you packing if you do," Andreas warned. "Lotte is her goddaughter; her mother was our cook for years before I was born."

"Oh, I'm only joking about her. But how about that little blonde who brings your mother honey and eggs?"

Andreas laughed delightedly to think of Heinz courting an ill-favored peasant girl who weighed about two hundred pounds. "I'm sure she already has her eye on you. She would make a passionate lover, just what you need."

"I'll let you know," said Heinz as they took the trail back, enlivened by the thought of inviting unknown pleasures.

The next day they stayed at home and Andreas got his father to draw them a map of the Obersalzburg area with directions to the cave. He sketched in the fences and roads of the Führer's mountain retreat as he remembered them from brief official visits before the war. The boys planned another day in the forest, with a visit to the cave. They even tried to coax Herr Wendel to go with them, but he claimed he was too old and stiff in the joints for capering around on mountain slopes. But they insisted he go with them to a band concert in town that evening, and he agreed.

The resort town lay huddled on a plain surrounded by the overbearing mountain landscape, its streets and houses clustered together around the fine old Gothic church. Neat squares alternated with sedate old streets and rows of shops. The concert was to be held in a picturesque old square near the outskirts of town; trees were neatly spaced around it and a little wooden bandstand stood in the middle. Colored lights were strung along one side in the lower branches of the trees, and open cafés vied with enclosed beer gardens for the summer clientele. Heinz and Andreas strolled through the crowd, remarking on the girls they passed, hoping to provoke a blush or an angry toss of the head. Andreas' parents had found seats in a café and ordered ices, and after a polite interval the boys left them there, already deep in local gossip.

When the boys were taking a last stroll around the green, a woman who looked vaguely familiar approached Heinz, loudly greeting him as Adam Leski. Luckily she spoke in Polish, so it was unlikely that anyone who heard her understood. He recognized her then, as a German teacher in the girls' high school in Katowice. She was asking volubly about the tragedy in his village and the fate of his family.

Heinz answered in Polish, for there was no disguising his Polish accent in German. "Madame, you are mistaking me for someone else. My name is Hauptmann, and I have never been in Polansk in my life." He bowed his best formal bow and, murmuring "Forgive me, madame, my hosts are expecting me," hurried on before she could contradict him.

Andreas was waiting at the next corner. "What did that old biddy want?" he inquired. "My mother hates her. She thinks she is a spy."

Heinz was more shaken by that piece of news than by the unexpected encounter. "She thought she knew me. Evidently she has lived in Poland."

"She has lived everywhere. Latvia, Czechoslovakia. She used to be a registry clerk in Salzburg, and now she has all kinds of jobs abroad and all kinds of money to spend. Her brother lives here all year round; he breeds dogs. She went to high school with my aunt. She was the one we saw on the station platform when we arrived."

Heinz breathed a sigh of relief. "Well, let's forget her then," he said and hastened his step toward the café where the Wendels were still sitting, talking animatedly.

Just before the concert was to start, a German officer addressed the crowd, with news of the war effort. He was tall and blond and spoke with a harsh precision that sent a chill through Heinz. The crowd greeted his reports of German advances with enthusiasm, buzzing with excitement; an occasional "Heil Hitler!" echoed through the small square. The anger which had become a part of Heinz's life possessed him. He did not hear the music but, as the gentle sounds filled the evening, grew firm in his resolve to have revenge.

As they walked home after the concert, Heinz offered Frau Wendel his arm in a burst of gallantry. He felt a sudden rush of affection for a woman whose hospitality would help fulfill his dream.

After his confrontation with the teacher, Heinz avoided the village and other public places where he was likely to encounter people. He favored solitary strolls with Andreas and parlor games with the Wendels on rainy days. He enjoyed looking through old albums of photographs and postcards, and often asked Frau Wendel to tell him about the places in them. He grew close to the Wendels, who were grateful for the friendship he gave their son.

One rainy day when the two boys were exploring the attic storeroom and listening surreptitiously to the erotic sounds of Lotte taking a bath next door, Heinz found a canvas-covered case with a familiar shape. "What is this?" he asked, extricating it from under an empty hatbox and a pile of old magazines and sheet music. "A trombone?" Andreas sighed and sat back on his heels, then looked down meditatively at his hands as if reluctant to answer.

"May I?" Heinz pressed him, motioning as though to open the catch. A rusted key hung from a string around the handle.

"It was my brother's," Andreas said finally.

"Oh. I didn't know you had a brother," Heinz exclaimed. He stopped in surprise. He waited for Andreas to get his courage together, for he was clearly upset at the turn the conversation had taken.

"He is really my half brother," Andreas explained, lowering his voice as though it were a secret. "My father was married before, and his wife ran away. She left my brother behind. His name is Klaus." Andreas paused for a moment, then plunged on: "He was five when I was born. He studied engineering in Vienna. See all those journals?"

Heinz looked at the stack of magazines more closely. They were professional journals of metallurgy.

"My mother brought them all back here when . . ." Andreas stopped and took a deep breath, then did not continue. Heinz did not press him, but sat silent listening to the pine branches sweeping the shingled roof.

"He was arrested," Andreas said flatly. His fists were clenched, his knuckles white.

"Oh, how dreadful!" said Heinz in quick sympathy. "How awful for your parents. Your father. I mean, is your mother fond of him? Of course she must be. What a terrible thing!" Heinz could not stop himself from babbling. The news of this family tragedy, so well contained and stoically borne, caught him unawares.

"I'm not supposed to know the reason, but he got in trouble over something political; it was due to the bad influence of friends. He was nineteen when it happened. Nobody's supposed to know it," he went on painfully, compulsively. "They're always watching me, too. For fear I might do the same." Andreas spread his hands out in a helpless gesture. "I only hope the Army will take me," he added, somewhat illogically.

Heinz forgot all about the canvas case. His friend's confession had shaken him. He longed to confide his own terrible secret, but he knew he must bear the burden of his dangerous impersonation alone. "Everyone seems to live with some hidden tragedy," he said, somewhat melodramatically. Andreas took it as an allusion to the death of Heinz's parents—which came close to the truth.

"You can open it," Andreas said, his hands on the case. "It's Klaus's crossbow. He used to be a champion, shooting in competitions. He was rated master arbalester—that's very good. It's a kind of snob sport, not many people care about it."

"My father used to have one," Heinz said excitedly. He realized he must be cautious, and wondered if the late Richard Hauptmann could safely be allowed this eccentricity. "He mostly hunted with it. I even used it myself."

"Well, I'll ask Mutti if we can take it down. I don't see why not. You don't have to know where Klaus is or why to borrow his crossbow, I guess. They'll tell you it was my uncle's, probably."

"Of course," said Heinz as he excitedly opened the case. Inside was a handsome Belgian crossbow with an inlaid stock. He lifted it from the case with tenderness, remembering how his father, meticulous about all his possessions and proud of having the husbandry of precious things, had cared for a much plainer weapon. "This must be an antique," Heinz said admiringly. "I could shine it up and oil it—look how rusty the prod is. And its catch is broken, look here." He rattled the broken part. "It's a beauty, though." He caressed the beautifully finished wood. "The breech needs a lot of work; it has to be as smooth as a gun barrel or the bolt can swerve off course. God, what a beauty!" He turned it over and over.

"I'll ask Mutti," Andreas promised. "You could teach me. We'll set up a target below the house in the woods." He had caught Heinz's enthusiasm. "We could buy a target in Salzburg. We could get the missing parts, too. I know a shop that sells guns and things like that."

After a few whispered family conferences, the boys were given possession of the crossbow. They made a special trip to

Salzburg to fit it with a new catch and trigger and buy a regulation target and new bolts. The storekeeper was impressed with the beautiful piece. "You know you could get a hundred marks for that, son. Maybe more," he volunteered. "I'd give you that much myself, if you ever decide to part with it. Don't treat it rough, now. You've got a collector's item there," he admonished them.

The boys thanked him and stayed on to admire tennis rackets and a case full of fishermen's flies, then made their way back to the railroad station. The streets were full of old men in dark suits and Tyrolean hats, young men in uniform, and women in colorful summer dresses rushing about the streets carrying bundles. It seemed festive, more like an operetta stage than a real city in a country at war. The cafés were full and the pace was unhurried. It was a victorious country, after all, one whose armies had vanquished its neighbors on every side and humbled the vainglorious French. The boys tasted victory in the air without knowing what it was, and they quickened their step, anxious to get down to the important task ahead.

This atmosphere of victory prevailed throughout the summer. Germany had already conquered not only France but Poland, Belgium, Holland, Denmark, and Norway. These victories were achieved with small losses. Each campaign took only a few weeks. The last enemy, England, could be conquered soon according to the headlines in the newspapers and speeches broadcast daily. The war would soon be over.

The summer went quickly by. Heinz was asked to stay on until school opened in the fall, and he wrote dutifully to his bank to forward his allowance once again to Rabenden. The boys practiced with the crossbow until they became quite proficient. Heinz could shoot a pine cone down from a high branch; he hit the target so well and so often that its face tore apart and came off. Andreas, although less skilled, was a keen sportsman. Uncompetitive by nature, he nevertheless enjoyed the tense power of the cocked string, the swift clean flight of the bolt, and the vibrant thwack it made as it hit its mark.

Just before they had to go back to school they took a day's excursion to Berchtesgaden to look for the cave. Using Herr Wendel's map, they followed a dry stream bed down the mountain until they were almost under the frail suspension bridge. It was broken now, obviously unused for a number of years. The boys had to climb the steep slope, scaling the rocks, then follow a narrow path that was all but obliterated by the forest growth. Then they found the cave's mouth, hidden by the hazel and elderberry bushes that grew thick at the foot of a sheer drop in the mountain's flank. Birds flew up in surprise as the boys entered the cave. The passage was damp and narrow, not at all as romantic as Andreas remembered it. They came to a widening of the passage, then to a large vaulted space with a trench of stagnant water along one side. There were dark piles of charred wood where someone had built fires, apparently long ago from the look of it.

"I wonder if this is the only entrance, or does it go on and on and come out somewhere else?" Heinz asked as they emerged into the light.

"As far as I know that's all there is," Andreas said. "It's not a very interesting cave, but people used to come here for walks or picnics. There were no bushes or brambles then; this was a clearing. The view was famous." The boys pushed their way through the thick growth to the edge of a steep drop-off, startling birds and stirring up brown grasshoppers as they went. A blue vista of mountains and valleys hung in the middle air between mists and sky, unreal as a stage backdrop.

The beauty of the scene below them silenced them both. Andreas was the first to speak. "How nice to have a house right here."

"You could live in the cave and be a hermit," suggested Heinz.

"Next summer we'll come and camp here. We could stay in that cave for a week and nobody would find us," said Andreas, suddenly animated.

"Why should they want to find us?" Heinz asked.

"It's state property. No camping allowed is why."

"I wouldn't chance it then," said Heinz, out of character. "Too much risk if you get caught."

"Well, we could camp somewhere else," said Andreas. He was begging some assurance that Heinz would come back next year.

"How about going to the Konigsee? There must be some good spots there," Heinz answered in tacit acknowledgment of his friend's question. It was like a pact between them. They would spend the next summer together.

They started back through the forest in silence, musing on the delicate bond they had forged. It was the first friendship Heinz had allowed himself since he left Poland. The fragile moment when they had stood on the edge of the void reaching out to each other wordlessly reminded him of how he had stood quaking after Lilka had kissed him and run up the stairs before he could recapture his wits. He wondered how Andreas felt about the Jews, about Poland, the war—indeed, about a great many things. There were stumbling blocks in friendship, he realized, that one scarcely dared to face. He set aside doubts for another day. He knew he would have to ponder whether he could permit himself the luxury of having a friend, and how much of himself was his to give in friendship.

Andreas had no such hesitations. He had never had a friend in all his shy, protected boyhood except Klaus, whom he had lost. Now he saw that it was very simple, no doubt like having a brother. He began to whistle, and birds called back.

In the train from Berchtesgaden the boys met an elderly Bavarian with a long pipe and a white beard. In the course of conversation he mentioned that at one time he had worked on the Obersalzburg in the Hotel Türken. This was before the war, before 1933, when the hotel had been closed and converted into lodgings for the SS men.

"Obersalzburg used to be a beautiful place," said the man. "All very distinguished people. Now all the property has been expropriated." The man spoke with obvious regret.

"I remember still, when the house the Führer bought was called Wachenfeld; now it is called Berghof. We used to walk around it. It had beautiful views. Now he has one hundred apiaries with honey bees; gone are the elegant ladies and gentlemen; only SS are around." The man spit out some tobacco, wiping the mouthpiece of his pipe on his leather shorts.

"Barbed wire all over the place. Guard dogs, watch towers. The beauty is gone."

As Heinz listened to the old man speak, he thought of the large trees that lined the electrified fence around Berghof, and of the crossbow, beautiful in shape, and deadly in purpose.

VIII

May 1941

Heinz perched himself carefully among the branches of the trees surrounding the electrified fence. He was hidden by the thick leaves, but occasionally the wind parted them and sent moonlight into his hiding place. His heart raced, beads of perspiration appeared on his brow, and he breathed deeply. His mind focused on the horrible vision of Hitler—the bust in the library, the countless posters and paintings in every public building in Germany. For a year he had devoted himself to his mission, training himself to use the crossbow he had stolen from the Wendels' attic, and now he sought inspiration from his hatred.

The complex consisted of five buildings, plain boxlike structures, to which the moon gave a blue tint. From one of the buildings he heard the raucous sound of singing, which disappeared with an echo into the night. Through the window of another he saw several officers bent over a table surveying a map.

There was a solitary dog barking in the distance. Below him Heinz could see a thick ground fog, and crossed himself in thanks. But his mission was murder, and the gesture was more out of habit than devotion.

Below him and about fifty yards to his right was a Nazi guard, and Heinz heard the crunching of the gravel under his boots. He worked his way forward on the branch until he was directly over the fence, and searched the trees on the far side for a sturdy limb that could withstand his weight. He satisfied himself with his choice and inched forward. When he could go no farther, he took a deep breath and jumped into the darkness. It seemed forever that he was suspended in midair, but he landed skillfully on the other tree, spreading his weight out over several different branches, using the strong but elastic limbs as a sort of trampoline. But still there was a crack as one of the small dead branches broke off and fell. It landed on the electric fence with a hiss and bounced off. Heinz looked quickly over to the guard, who had turned toward the tree and looked up. He held his breath as the guard took three steps toward him and twisted his head, peering up into the tree. Heinz breathed slowly and deeply when the guard turned, lit a cigarette, and headed back toward the far end of the compound.

Quickly Heinz swung down from the tree, hanging by his arms, and dropped to the ground. He landed quietly, the crossbow and poisoned bolts still lashed firmly to his back. He crouched low and ran silently across the small yard to the side of one of the buildings, and hid himself, behind a small shed. Suddenly there appeared from a building on the other side of the yard a jeep whose lights illuminated the corner of his hiding place. He flattened himself against the building; the light cast his shadow on the adjoining wall, but the jeep drove away and he heard the two soldiers in it arguing good-naturedly.

He crawled along the ground. He knew he was near the field in front of Hitler's house. When he reached the shelter of a bush, he raised his head and saw the wall of a building only one hundred meters away.

Slowly he raised himself to a kneeling position. His eyes discerned a group of figures on the terrace. Then Heinz suddenly recognized the man: Adolf Hitler. Heinz shuddered. He had to lie down again, his heart quaking wildly. He did not know how long it took to regain control of himself, but when he returned to the kneeling position, Hitler was still clearly visible on the terrace.

Heinz took out a bolt, his fingers quivering. He readied the poisoned arrow. His blood was pounding and he felt a profound joy as he looked over the sight of the crossbow.

Suddenly from out of the darkness on his left came a low growl, and as he turned he saw a large German shepherd flying through the air toward him. The dog attacked him fiercely, knocking the crossbow out of his hands and biting first his right arm and then his stomach. Heinz struggled with the strong animal as he felt his strength waning and the dog overcoming him. Finally, he managed to get hold of one of the poisoned arrows, and with his last bit of strength plunged it into the dog's side. The dog whimpered, and in a matter of seconds gave up the attack, lay timidly on its side and died. Heinz looked up frantically to see if they had heard the struggle but the night wind and animated conversation had covered the sounds. He thought of rushing up and stabbing Hitler with an arrow, but his strength was gone and he was bleeding. He might be thwarted. So with the hope of a future opportunity, and the image of the devil burning in his brain, he retreated.

A large truck was leaving a garage and Heinz positioned himself by the side of the driveway that led from the camp. When the truck passed, Heinz leaped on the back of it, and hid himself under the canvas hood. When the truck had passed safely through the gates, he jumped out, hitting the ground hard, and rolled into a gully by the side of the road.

He had left the crossbow and arrows behind.

IX

May 1941

Herr Piersohn looked at the bench and hesitated for a moment as if he were not sure whether the wooden planks comprising the seating facilities in the Englischer Garten would withstand the weight of his body. Lowering himself gingerly, he made a face as if he were throwing himself into icy waves. The bench squeaked a bit but Herr Piersohn remained safely seated at its center.

After this effort Herr Piersohn decided to take off his homburg and put it at his side. He also took out of his breast pocket a neatly folded handkerchief and wiped away the drops of perspiration that had accumulated on his forehead. It was still breezy this mid-May noon in Munich, but he was not used to walking outdoors much. Fresh air tired him easily. After he finished drying his forehead, he remained seated without moving. He did not want to push his luck with the bench too far. Fortunately, he did not have to wait long before Harimann arrived. Before Herr Piersohn could get up the newcomer was seated.

"You were not followed?" Harimann asked.

"No, I don't think so."

"Fine, I have come to talk to you. . . . I will need your services. Listen carefully! Don't interrupt! I have not much time." He took off his horn-rimmed glasses and put them into the side pocket of his tweed jacket.

"I may have found the man we need. It appears that an inexperienced and daring adventurer, acting alone and possessing extraordinary prowess, planned an attempt on the Führer's life and failed. The following findings have led me to this hypothesis:

"On May 10 when I was visiting the Eagle's Nest, I came across the body of a dead dog. It was a female German Shepherd, belonging to the SS Guards of the *Leibstandarte*. The body was in the bushes in front of the building complex." Harimann stopped, clearing his throat. During his monologue he did not look at Piersohn. He looked beyond, perhaps somewhere into the future. Piersohn made a motion, expecting that Harimann's silence was an invitation to ask questions, but Harimann noticed Piersohn's lips ready to speak and waved his hand to silence him.

"The cause of death was an arrow, of the type used in crossbow shooting. I removed the arrow, wrapped it in my handkerchief, and took it to a chemist whom I trust to analyze it for poison."

"It could have been Reichsmarschall Göring," Piersohn said. "He is a known hunter. But perhaps a soldier . . ."

"No, it could only be an outsider. I discovered in the area, not far from the dead dog, a broken branch on the ground beneath a fir tree. Another newly severed branch was hanging from a trunk two meters from ground level. I observed other broken branches. From these findings I deduced that somebody must have been jumping from tree to tree. The dog must have surprised him. Climber and archer must have been the same person."

"Remarkable!" Piersohn said, pulling out of his pocket a leather cigar case.

"No one has ever penetrated the enclosed precinct," Harimann said. "This man must have been something of an acrobat as well as a marksman."

"Was this man alone?" Piersohn asked.

"There are many mysteries surrounding that exploit. I don't know the answers . . . not yet."

"Did somebody else notice?"

"No, Herr Piersohn." Harimann put his glasses back on. "Everyone was preoccupied with the flight of Deputy Führer Hess to Britain. Hitler was in a rage. I buried the dog far off in the woods, hoping to conceal the assassination attempt. This man may well be valuable to us. Were it not for the dog, he surely would have succeeded."

"How do we find him?"

"That exactly is the reason I am seeing you now, my dear Herr Piersohn. This will be your task."

Piersohn almost lost the cigar. "But how, Herr Harimann? How?"

"There is more to my story, Herr Piersohn. Next to the dog's body was the crossbow that the assassin carried. There was blood around the dog's mouth; she must have attacked the assassin and driven him off. Start by checking any stores that handle crossbows and accessories," he said as he handed Piersohn a large package wrapped in plain brown paper.

"I will give you ten days. We will meet on May 20 in Bad Reichenhall."

"Hotel Deutscher Kaiser?" Piersohn asked.

"Oh no, on Predigstuhl, on top of one of the peaks." Harimann smiled. "You don't have to worry, Herr Piersohn, about climbing it on foot. There is an aerial railway."

The prospect of dangling in the air did not improve Piersohn's humor.

"At eleven o'clock in the morning you will find me sunbathing in one of the easy chairs. A chair next to mine will be free." Harimann cleared his throat. "Have a good day, or should I say a good ten days." Harimann turned around and strode away while Piersohn collected his homburg and moved his bulky body in the opposite direction.

Heinz made his way back to the Oberschule, arriving at 4 A.M., and presented himself to Kotecha at the infirmary. He had to trust Kotecha, his wounds badly needed treatment. He made up an elaborate story of being attacked by a wolf, but he knew from the beginning that the old Czech did not believe him. Kotecha looked at him with compassion as he dressed the wounds.

"Wolves are very dangerous animals," he said. "It is said they are haunted by the spirits of the dead," he continued while slowly wrapping Heinz's wrist with gauze. He winced as Kotecha cleaned out a small wound on his hand and gave him a shot to protect him against rabies.

"Now off with you to bed," Kotecha said. "There's a general inspection in three hours, you'd better be there."

From the look in Kotecha's eyes he knew he had nothing to fear.

"You won't tell anybody, will you?" he said.

"I'm a medic, not a policeman," Kotecha answered.

When the alarm sounded, Heinz had a vague memory of falling asleep. He was still in his clothes, and had a slight feeling of nausea and a headache. His hand hurt and he remembered Kotecha when he saw the bandage on his wrist. The other boys looked at him curiously, but dared not tease him. They remembered that his aunt was sick—he had invented the illness to get a three-day absence—and until they knew she was all right, Heinz was exempt from the raillery at which the boys were so expert.

The morning was cool and crisp. The boys formed in groups in the schoolyard and awaited Herr Harimann, who was to perform inspection and speak to them about the military fortunes of the Third Reich. When Harimann appeared from the building that housed his office, a brief buzz went through the crowd of boys and they quickly snapped to attention.

Heinz was overcome with fatigue and pain as he stood in line between Andreas and Heinrich Stroebe. As Harimann made his way through the ranks of boys, Heinz thought again of that moment of wild joy when his crossbow was trained on the terrace. Were it not for that dog Hitler would be dead. In the clear morning, as Harimann inspected the uniforms and bearing of the Hitler Youth, Heinz reaffirmed his oath to kill Hitler. Unknown to him, so did the headmaster of the Oberschule.

Finally, Harimann arrived in front of Heinz.

"Good morning, Hauptmann," he said. "Herr Neufeind told me you had requested a three-day leave. We didn't expect you back until this evening."

He extended his hand in greeting and said, "I'm sorry to hear about your aunt. I hope she's all right." Heinz reached out and shook his hand. "She's much better, sir. Thank you," he said. Harimann looked down and saw the wound on Heinz's hand. "Nasty wound," he said. "I'd have Kotecha take a look at that."

"Yes, sir. Thank you, sir," Heinz mumbled. He knew he had made a second terrible error—the first had been leaving behind the crossbow.

May 20 turned out to be a cloudy day in Bad Reichenhall. On the Predigstuhl, however, the sun managed to appear from time to time between the clouds and light the faces of the few sunbathers. Piersohn recognized Harimann despite the sun glasses he was wearing. He was lying in an easy chair some twenty meters away from the other sunbathers. Seeing Piersohn, Harimann motioned him to lie down on the empty chair next to his.

"I prefer standing, Herr Harimann."

"Any results?" Harimann asked.

"Yes. I followed your suggestion, Herr Harimann." Piersohn opened his cigar case.

"Don't you dare to pollute the mountain air with your smelly cigars!"

Piersohn obediently closed his cigar case. "They are the best Brazil cigars. . . . Anyway, in an orbit of one hundred kilometers around Berchtesgaden there are only three stores where crossbows are sold—one is in Rabenden, two in Salzburg. The store in Rabenden reported three sales of crossbows in the past year; Klingelein's in Salzburg made two sales, the other made none."

Piersohn looked down and discovered that he was standing

only a few meters away from a precipice. His head began to spin. Holding on to the chair, he sat down on the bare rock.

"I really . . . would prefer meeting you in restaurants . . . I am not very good, not here in the mountains."

Harimann smiled. "With good results, next time we will meet again in a place like the Hotel Imperiale."

"Where were we?" Piersohn said. "Oh, yes. I showed the crossbow to all of the dealers, and the one in Rabenden recognized it immediately. He said that two Hitler Youth had been in his shop last year, looking for parts for it. In fact, he admired the weapon so much he tried to buy it from them."

Harimann rose from his chair, and Piersohn, seeing Harimann so absorbed in his story, put the cigar in his mouth and, without resorting to his normal routine of cutting the cigar, bit off the end with his teeth and lighted it, blowing the smoke in the direction of the precipice.

The hard rock on which he was sitting pressed against his heavy body. He changed position and continued, "I thought perhaps it had been some of the students at your school. The man said that it was during the summer that the boys had been in his shop, so I made inquiries in the vicinity to find out if any of the parents of your boys live in the area of Rabenden."

"Yes, yes, and what did you find out?" Harimann screamed, annoyed at the slowness with which Piersohn was talking. Piersohn, on the other hand, was enjoying drawing out the story. For once he knew something Harimann was desperate to hear.

"There is a boy named Andreas Wendel in your school and his parents live in Rabenden. I visited them at their home, and they freely admitted that the crossbow was theirs, but said that it had been stolen. They hadn't missed it until two months ago, but agreed it may have been gone for some time. The last time they had seen it was last summer, when Andreas and his friend Heinz Hauptmann, who was a summer guest, had asked for permission to use it."

Harimann was agitated. "Hauptmann is also a boy from the Oberschule, isn't he?" he asked Piersohn, slightly embarrassed at having to ask an outsider about his school. He paced back and forth in front of Piersohn, who puffed contentedly on his cigar.

"Yes he is, Herr Harimann. And according to Neufeind he was absent from school from May 9 until the morning of May 11. If that's not enough proof, how's this?" said Piersohn confidently. "The morning of the twelfth he was treated in the infirmary for a wound on his hand. A dog bite, perhaps?"

"There's no doubt, he's our man," said Harimann, looking directly at Piersohn. "You will have to contact him, Piersohn. Report back to me." With this he stormed back toward the aerial railway station, leaving Piersohn to reflect on the fact that he had not received the slightest congratulations for his findings. When he looked up Harimann was standing over him again.

"You're a fool, Piersohn" he said. "The school was the one place where you shouldn't have asked questions." He watched as Harimann left again, this time boarding a rail car and heading down the mountain.

After a reasonable time, he got up and went down the mountain to find the boy who wanted Hitler dead.

X

June 1941

On the morning of June 22, when the boys had assembled for breakfast, Rüger arrived and requested them to stand at attention.

"The moment all of us have been secretly hoping for has arrived," Rüger said. "Our Führer has ordered our soldiers to invade Russia. There will be no classes today. Now the Führer speaks."

The boys remained standing at attention while the well-known voice of Adolf Hitler, amplified by loudspeakers of the radio, spoke:

"I can only now speak freely. The greatest march in history is taking place now. Victory will be total." He concluded, "I have decided again to place the fate of the Reich and our people in the hands of our soldiers. May God aid us, especially in this fight!"

Heinz closed his eyes. Only a few weeks ago he had had the

chance to silence this voice forever. This voice, ordering a new mass murder of innocent people. How many mothers like his would be tortured to death! How many families like his would be destroyed!

When Rüger ordered them to sit down, Heinz remained standing until Andreas pulled him down.

At breakfast the boys spoke of the new campaign with enthusiasm. Most of them expected the victory within a few weeks and expressed regret not to be able to participate in this "victory march."

After breakfast the school assembled in the hall to listen to more radio broadcasts. Various speakers talked about the viciousness of the enemy and the inhumanity of the people in the Soviet Union. Later on Rüger told them about the Jews dominating Soviet Russia. "We will kill all of them," he said. "The land will be ours. We don't need these people. We will get rid of them. The German farmer will take over the good soil of Russia and Ukraine and will increase the agricultural production. This will also be the end of communism."

But Heinz did not listen. He dreamed the Germans would be repulsed. According to the news the next few days, however, they seemed to move quickly into Russia. Heinz knew he must develop a new plan.

XI

Summer 1941

At the end of that school year, several students at the Oberschule in Nyphelheim were leaving for the Army, the Navy, or the Air Force. There were already four names engraved under the eagle and swastika emblem on a marble panel of the entrance to the reception hall. It was a large panel; in fact the whole entry was walled with bare marble slabs. Every boy who passed must have wondered at some idle moment whether his own name would figure there before the victory was won.

Heinz had persuaded Andreas to go with him to Munich for the first part of the vacation. They planned to room in a student boarding house and explore the city. There would be movies, cafés, dance halls, adventures, and curiosities beyond their imaginings; Andreas would write poems, sketches of life in the wartime city; he could talk to soldiers who had been at the front and write their recollections. Heinz had studies to make, strategies to devise. Besides, he was not eager to go back to Rabenden, where the missing crossbow was sure to have caused a scandal.

The boys took a train that arrived in Munich in the early evening. The city was glowing in a golden half-light; the sun reflected red in the polished window panes of the Karlsplatz. They found two tiny rooms in an old house in the Schwabing and went out to roam the streets.

Andreas jauntily lit a cigarette as they walked along, drunk on their newly acquired freedom. They had had to smoke in secret up until now, hiding in the bathrooms or behind the guardhouse in the woods. They decided to go to a movie to test their new station in life—no curfew, no light-out-no-more-talking, no silent proctor checking each bed to see that clothes were neatly hung, books neatly stacked, shoes neatly aligned, and the occupant neatly inserted under the covers. The movie was a complicated love story with a happy ending, called "Wunschkonzert." The boys were more fascinated by their own presence in the dark theater, surrounded by strangers, than by anything they saw on the screen. They went home to their dingy rooms and talked excitedly through the open door between them until it was nearly dawn.

During the first week they explored the city, sometimes together, sometimes separately. Andreas liked to sit in a café near the railway station and watch the travelers—soldiers arriving, alone and faceless, or in large, laughing, jostling groups like small boys let out of class. Some were met by their sweethearts and they stood shamelessly kissing each other until he had to look away. He was keeping a detailed diary and writing long letters to his parents almost daily.

In Munich, everywhere, in storewindows and in public offices, large maps of the Soviet Union were displayed. Each map showed hundreds of small flags with swastikas marking the progress of the German conquest. Andreas would stop, admire the speed of the German Army's forward movement. For Heinz, each transfer of a swastika pin meant hundreds of thousands of hostages killed, villages burned, millions displaced. When Andreas started to talk about the war and German victories, Heinz tried to change the subject.

Heinz took walks to memorize the city streets; he wandered past landmarks hallowed by the new mythology of National Socialism. With a lover's obsessive fascination, he traced the steps of the man he meant to kill. He went to the Haus der Deutschen Kunst almost every day to study the portraits of the Führer, the mementos of the Party's historic acts. He steeped himself in loathing until he reached a kind of exaltation in which his daydream of murder seemed close to realization.

In the museum Heinz was making a sketch of Adolf Hitler's face from a portrait by Ulrich Grote. The boy's devotion to the Führer had been perceived by the guards, but it was not the first example of such hero worship they had witnessed. Many a lad whose older comrades had marched victorious into France or sailed into Norwegian ports longed to be with the armies now advancing in the East. They had been reared from childhood on the dream of German conquest of the subhuman Slavs; now the Führer's genius had brought all Europe under the red and black banner of the Fatherland. Those who were too young to fight the final battles and taste the ultimate victories came to this shrine of Nazism like old women to church. They only hoped the war would last long enough for them to be heroes or to die for the Führer and the Fatherland. The old guards, one of them a one-legged victim of the other great war, read the signs of daydreaming in the boys' mannered swagger, their absorption in the warlike displays, their look of having just fallen in love. Heinz was not like them; he was more methodical but just as faithful and intense.

An older man, a frequent visitor, strolled past and looked over Heinz's shoulder at the sketch. One guard nudged the other.

"A good likeness, yes, very good," said the man. Heinz looked around into the protuberant blue eyes of a stout, gray-haired man, slightly shorter than he, with a neatly groomed mustache. The man smiled, bowing somewhat affectedly.

"Permit me to remark," he added. He wore gold-rimmed glasses and held a homburg and fine gray gloves in one hand.

Heinz acknowledged the compliment with a nervous murmur and went back to his contemplation, but the man did not move on. Perhaps he was an art professor, or a collector, a connoisseur. Heinz was not drawing the portrait to exercise his talent, but to focus his meditation. He had made three sketches already and taken them home to mutilate and eventually to burn. It was a ritual he felt had great efficacy; a worn little secondhand book he had bought in the Schwabing told of the strange powers of images when inspired with concentrated purpose and desire. When he drew the eyes and brushed in the deep shadows, a strange familiarity chilled him; each time it was the same, as though he had gazed into those eyes at close quarters and felt a cold shaft glance off the edge of consciousness, like a touch of foulness from beyond the grave.

"You are at the Akademie der Kunst?" asked the man. "Talented, yes indeed, very talented."

"No, sir," said Heinz. "And I am not talented at all." He closed his sketch pad and began to gather up his charcoals.

"Tut-tut-tut-tut-tut," said the man. "Don't let an old lover of art frighten you away. Youth has its pride. I know it well. Artists are a proud breed. Oh, I should know, I should know." The man rocked back and forth, lost in his mysterious recollections. Before Heinz could take a step, he went on, "I knew Grote as a young man. Ah, yes. There was a superb talent. Proud as a Turk. Proud as a jungle beast. Come now, say you're not put out." He was blocking Heinz's escape, teetering back and forth on his shiny black shoes. Heinz noted with amazement that he wore spats.

"No, indeed, of course not. Forgive me, sir. I have to go." He could not decently push the man aside, yet he would not budge.

"That portrait of Herr Hitler. Now, it's not the best one to copy. A good likeness, but bland. No fire. The Führer, now, has fire. Power. Energy waves, vibrations like an electric storm when he speaks. Now, you don't have to show them in the picture, but you have to put them in the viewer's mind. This man is a great genius, a shaper of destiny." The fat man looked inquiringly at Heinz through his thick lenses. "Do you follow my thought?"

"Yes, sir," said Heinz. He was trapped, he knew, but the man began to intrigue him. "You really knew Grote?"

"Oh, indeed, intimately. *Intimately*. Before his death, he sent me a message. I knew it meant he would take his own life."

"But he was drowned in an accident," Heinz said. He had just read the artist's biography posted near the portrait.

The fat man smiled knowingly and flapped his gloves against his homburg.

"You mean . . . it was not an accident?" Heinz was astounded.

"An arranged accident. He did not want to give his enemies the satisfaction of his despair," the man said delicately.

"But his friend drowned too."

"It was agreed between them," said the man. "That was what the message to me meant. I knew his friend well. A brilliant student." He sighed. "Art is a calling not to be entered on lightly," he remarked with a smug, knowing air. "Our Führer is an artist," he said then, looking down at his hat. They stood in silence contemplating this mystery.

"Our Führer is a genius," said Heinz then. He suddenly wanted to talk about Adolf Hitler, to hear this strange old man tell all he knew or could invent.

Piersohn told Heinz that he was a draftsman in a firm of architects; that he also gave private English lessons. Heinz replied that he was studying English in school and gave a sample of his mastery, but Herr Piersohn did not pursue the subject. He was expatiating on his life of painting. ". . . a pity that the Pinakothek was closed just after the war broke out," he said. "I used to spend hours there. Happy tranquil hours." He stopped walking to reflect on his lost tranquility, absently patting Heinz's arm. "There were enough beautiful paintings to keep one in ecstasy for days on end." He sighed and moved on toward the English garden. Heinz was waiting to bring the subject back to the genius of the Führer, but Herr Piersohn wanted to talk about Murillo. "There were two darling little paintings, no, three. Little Spanish beggar boys with their rags falling off their adorable round shoulders. Exquisite. They looked innocent and quite, quite helpless; their big eyes would follow you around the room. Delicious painter,

Murillo. You will see them someday. After the war our beauties will be returned to us." He patted Heinz reassuringly on the arm, as though he were the one mourning the eclipse of the beggar boys. "Don't you worry."

"After the victory," said Heinz automatically. No one ever said "After the war."

"Ah yes, you young worshipers at the shrine of Mars. You would like to be out there fighting for your Führer on the Eastern Front, I suppose?"

"Yes, sir, indeed," said Heinz. It would not do to say no; the man could be a Gestapo informer, although the idea seemed a bit ludicrous when one considered the homburg and gold-rimmed spectacles and spats.

"Yes, you would. Well, you may get your chance before this is over," said Piersohn.

"Our armies are going to be in Moscow before long," said Heinz. "Then it will be all over. We will build a New Order in Europe."

"So. And what will you be in the New Order? A painter? An artist?" Herr Piersohn's voice had a teasing note.

I shall be an assassin and never see the New Order, thought Heinz. He said, "Who knows? I think I should like to be a farmer. I only draw for fun. It is not serious."

"Well, good day, my lad. We shall meet again." Herr Piersohn tipped his homburg ceremoniously, as they were emerging from the garden into the street, and walked rapidly off. Heinz watched him bounce daintily through the crowd, jaunty and light on his feet. He saw him tip his hat to a burly, youngish man in a workman's leather jacket, who turned briskly and headed toward the garden. When he was nearly abreast of Heinz, he crossed the street and disappeared into the crowd.

Heinz took the sketch Piersohn had admired home to his room and, after locking himself in, changed it into the face of a corpse with staring eyes and hanging jaw, like the corpses of partisans he had once seen hanging from lamp posts in Poland outside the railway station in Sosnowice. He drew a rope around the neck and a dagger in the throat. Then he sat remembering things in the order in which they had happened: His father asking him if he'd like to go into Polansk the next day to look at a new cultivator he was thinking of getting; the rumor in Polansk that the Germans had invaded Poland. The sound of shooting; the village streets full of soldiers; his father and himself dragged out of the post office along with three other men; the afternoon in the church. The ride in the dim truck. The firing squad. At each step in his meditation, he accused the man before him, whom he had judged, sentenced, and executed. He put the sketch on the bed and stabbed it furiously over and over with a compass point. When the paper was in shreds, he gathered the scraps into a metal ash tray and put a match to them. He had learned to discipline himself to remain perfectly calm, to contain his fury until it was wound tight inside him like a spring. Then he would perform feats of strength—break wooden slats, bend metal rods, tear heavy strips of cardboard. He had found a gym where he could exercise every morning, lifting weights, punching a sandbag, and working out on parallel bars. But this dispassionate routine did not compare with the performances of rage. He told the coach at the gym, as well as Andreas and all who inquired, that he wanted to build up his strength so he would not be rejected from the Army because of his wounds or some weakness left in his lungs from his pneumonia. Andreas came to the gym from time to time. He, too, was afraid of rejection, but exercise bored him, and he often found an excuse instead to meet Heinz later in the café of the Hotel Der Kaiser near the railroad station, where he had a special table from which he could watch people and write his poems.

One day the two were eating lunch there—their lunch was often rye bread, jam, and tea—when Herr Piersohn appeared at their table with homburg and gray gloves in hand. To Heinz's surprise, Andreas greeted him as "Herr Professor," and then said in English, "Will you please join at our table?"

"With pleasure," rejoined Piersohn in English, making himself comfortable between them. "But you should not say 'join at our table' but 'join us at our table' or 'please sit at our table.' Ah, but you are making progress all the same. Practice. The secret is practice."

Andreas blushed with pleasure. "How I should like to know

English really well! Herr Piersohn, may I present my friend Heinz." To Heinz, he said, "Herr Piersohn is an English professor."

"We've met. In the museum." Heinz was surprised and somewhat put out. Then he remembered that Piersohn had told him he was an artist. Or a draftsman—it came to the same thing. If he met a butcher boy, he probably would say he was a butcher, reflected Heinz sourly. The older man was ordering more sweet buns and tea for the boys.

"So! The future of German arts and letters is assured," said Piersohn, settling back comfortably and sipping his tea. "Your friend Heinz here has talent," he said to Andreas. "He is no farmer. Did he show you his sketch of the Führer?"

"I tore it up," said Heinz. "It was not good. As you said, Herr Piersohn, it had no fire, no spirit. It is not easy to catch the Führer's aura. A likeness, yes, but not the essence, not the dynamism."

"Have you ever seen the Führer in person?" asked Piersohn. Both boys shook their heads. "In the old days one used to see him. Here in Munich. In the streets, in the cafés. But since the war he keeps to himself. He only appears on great occasions."

"He is afraid since Elser's bomb nearly killed him," said Andreas.

"I suppose it could happen again," said Herr Piersohn. He was drawing rings absent-mindedly on the tabletop. "But not in the same way. Now they look out for bombs and madmen like Elser. The Führer is protected day and night."

"A woman could kill him. Like Judith killed Holofernes. Sleep with him and kill him in bed," said Andreas. "She cut off Holofernes' head. Do you think any woman could do that nowadays?"

"All old Jewish rubbish," scoffed Piersohn, leaning close to Andreas and putting his hand on the boy's shoulder. He spoke softly, "Do you think *you* could kill someone after making love?"

Andreas was too embarrassed to answer. It repelled him for Herr Piersohn to dwell on the subject of his making love, a subject which, nonetheless, he himself gave a lot of thought to. Piersohn leaned back in his chair with an authoritative air. "Now, if I were an assassin, I would attack my victim in the most vulnerable situation. Not when he has a full regiment protecting him, but when his guards are few. For example, when he is traveling. In a motor car or train. That's when the physical limitations on guards are greatest. Particularly in a train—no outriders on motorcycles. I wouldn't count on getting him in bed." He chuckled somewhat bawdily and winked at Heinz. "Anybody who can think that would work doesn't realize that making love is fairly . . . ah . . . extenuating?" he added daintily. "Changes one's mind about stalwart deeds, murder, beheading, all that," he went on. "Momentarily."

In a car or on a train. That was something to think about. The Bürgerbräukeller of course was out after Elser's adventure. But a moving train . . .

Andreas and Herr Piersohn were deep in conversation about the Jewish fables of the Old Testament and their fascination down the ages. Piersohn affirmed that they were not invented by the same people as the Jews of today, who were a mongrel breed, vagabonds and parasites. He spoke of other mythologies, much more potent, too much so to be generally publicized. Andreas was patently intrigued by Piersohn's talk of initiates, of arcane knowledge, wakefulness of an order totally different from our daily dream-consciousness. The presence of secret masters among us appealed to his mystical nature. He forgot to drink his tea and let it get cold. Heinz wanted to tell them about Kotecha's fortune-telling cards with the four-leaf clover in a golden chalice, but decided against it. He had promised to keep the old nurse's secret.

When the three parted, it was with a promise to meet again. Piersohn strolled off down the Bayerstrasse, and Andreas caught a trolley to the Schwabing. Heinz remained; he went into the railway station to look at the trains. When at last he passed the Hotel Der Kaiser café on his way to the trolley stop, he glanced at the table where they had sat. Three men in Gestapo uniform and a civilian were sitting there drinking beer; he could see only one, who had a round, freckled face with sandy brows and bright red hair. The civilian turned his head slightly, and Heinz saw him in profile. It was Dietrich Rüger.

XII

Fall 1941–Winter 1942

Heinz returned from his summer in Munich with vague apprehensions about what might have passed between Andreas and Piersohn, between Andreas and his parents if the crossbow had been missed, between the Wendels and the police if it had been found. He did not dare to put any of these questions to his friend, and was confused that Andreas did not mention anything about the crossbow.

After classes started and the athletics program got under way, the two boys saw less of each other. Andreas spent long hours writing his diary and letters home, and seemed distant from Heinz. The casual intimacy that had developed between them that first summer gave way to a reserved, more formal relationship.

Heinz had changed too. He had grown taller and more muscular over the summer, and his acquaintance with independence and city life had lent an air of sophistication to his gait and gestures. His bland, still boyish features now and then reflected the shadows that haunted his mind. He resembled his mother now, fair and open-countenanced, his ready smile and high coloring distracting attention from the watchful, resolute gray eyes. Girls in the village began to look at him and giggle behind his back.

The first one bold enough to flirt was the pretty blond Trudi, daughter of a local baker. She waited on the boys when they piled into the shop on Sundays and watched to see if any of them struck her fancy. One day when Heinz was alone in the shop, she served him noticeably more than good measure, and invited him coyly to come back soon, hinting that with a bit of good will one could always stretch the ration coupons a little further than the law allowed. He wondered uneasily at this sudden bounty, and felt shy about returning. But Trudi, at sixteen, was experienced in flirtation, and soon afterward Heinz met her on the street just coming out of the bakery as he passed by. She accused him of avoiding her, and as he protested, confused, he found himself walking beside her toward a café, dazzled at the way she walked close to him and flashed her blond curls about her shoulders, at her teasing ways and funny local drawl. He was not sure of how to talk to girls who acted the way Trudi did, but she seemed pleased with whatever he said or did—as indeed she was. She was not accustomed to the fine manners and deference that were natural to a boy of Heinz's class and breeding, and she was excited at being in the company of a foreigner; Heinz was to her the very embodiment of a man of the world.

Trudi arranged their next meeting the same as she had the first, and soon Heinz fell into the habit of waiting for her on the corner across from her father's bakery whenever he went into town. At Christmas she gave him a poppy-seed cake, and, tardily, he brought her an amber brooch, like the ones he had often seen in Poland. She walked him to the edge of town and said goodbye under the arch of the gate. "I'll show you how they kiss in the movies," she offered and, before Heinz could collect himself, pressed her moist parted lips to his.

Embarrassed and confused at his own vertigo, he pulled away

from her and said a brisk good-bye and Merry Christmas. On the way back to school, he tried to recapture the moment, but the woman of his erotic dreams and the curly-headed, pink-faced Trudi would not merge into one. Trudi, on the other hand, had no such trouble. Heinz and the heroes of her cinema fantasy world were the same—shadowy masculine presences that served as a foil for her own glittering drama of expectancy and fulfillment. She hummed as she went about her work in the bakery and at home and fancied herself in love. When the pre-Lenten season of *Fasching*, with its celebrations, came around, she invited Heinz to a masquerade ball, promising to furnish him with a costume that her brother had left behind when he went off to work in a factory in Salzburg.

Heinz was to be a rather rustic demon and Trudi a winged spirit. When they arrived at the hall, it was already noisy and crowded. The room was lighted by crystal chandeliers. The elegant sound of a string quartet came from one room, and from another the gay oom-pah of a larger band. Trudi was swept away from him by a group of laughing friends who wanted to know all about her handsome escort and how she had lured him there. He found himself face to face with a dark-haired priestess or oriental queen in long purple robes with a golden scepter in one hand and a coronet of gold on her head. She had witnessed the abduction of his partner, and now smiled at his dismay. She touched his shoulder lightly with her wand and said, "Spirit, tell me who you are."

"I am the spirit that negates," said Heinz, taking her clue and feeling very pleased with himself. She was slim, taller than average, and no doubt even handsomer without her mask. She spoke with a northern accent, in a cultivated voice. "Then are you Liar, Destroyer, Lord of Flies?" she teased.

"Well," said Heinz, whose literary repertoire had been exhausted in one phrase, "I am very wicked, but tonight I am on my best behavior."

The music resumed, and to his own surprise, he bowed to invite her to dance. Being disguised exhilarated him; it was as though he could drop his habitual masquerade and be Adam

Leski, a forthright, high-spirited youth with no secrets to guard, no death sentence hanging over him. For Adam, *Fasching* was more than a license to flirt and play pranks and say bold and scandalous things to strangers: it was the world put right again—for an instant everyone's real identity was hidden so that his could go free. At the end of the dance he bowed over his partner's hand and said, "Thank you, Your Royal Highness," adding, "You are a queen, aren't you?"

"I am Queen of Fate," she answered.

A couple dressed in a similar style came rushing up to them. "Else," said a golden-robed empress, "come and have champagne."

His queen was gone as magically as she had appeared. He roamed about, looking vaguely for Trudi, as drunk on the lights and colors and gaiety as though he had had champagne himself. He danced with an elfin maiden all in green, who kept giggling but would not say a word; he drank a stein of beer handed to him by a tipsy knight in armor, and joined in a grand promenade arm in arm with a stout Brunhilde wearing braids down to her knees. Trudi finally reclaimed him and helped him find some supper and another glass of beer. She clung to him possessively and fed him sweets with her fingers, brushing her bright curls close to his face. Heinz found himself hoping, somewhat shamefacedly, that the stately Queen of Fate would not see him supping in affectionate familiarity with his coy woodland sprite.

In the dark hours of morning, he finally took Trudi home, kissed her soundly, as she was expecting him to, and left his demon clothes in the cold spare room behind the bakery. They breakfasted on hot ersatz coffee and sweet rolls, whispering and holding hands; then he left her and went toward the station to wait for a train back to the Oberschule.

To get to the platform, he had to cross an overpass where the railroad cut the town proper off from a somewhat shabby residential neighborhood, half town, half village. Warehouses and shops with unwashed windows lined the empty streets, which had a general air of abandonment. He stood watching a train pass by, just a meter or two beneath his feet. He wondered about despair and about people who throw themselves in front of trains. Then a sudden dizziness overpowered him as another train swept through without slowing down; he held on to the thin iron rail to prevent himself from vaulting the barrier and jumping—whether out of desire to be one with the strength and swiftness of the train or to make his frail body a sacrifice to the monstrous iron deity, he could not say. It was as strong an impulse as he had ever felt; he knew it was close to madness. Only when the train had passed did he dare to let go his grip and make his way down the steps to the platform. He felt himself shaking, possessed by a lust to do violence.

Standing as close to the platform's edge as he dared, he watched the trains come and go until Andreas hopped down from one and saluted him jovially. Heinz greeted him as though from a great distance. He was pale and shaking, from an exercise in concentration which, after his sleepless night, had brought him to a state of excitement and detachment like a fever delirium. The resonance of the great iron wheels, the beat of their pulse, the incessant repetition of light and shadow, and the stately, implacable rhythm gave him a sense of being on the verge of momentous revelations. He felt light-headed, invisible. He was exhilarated by the Queen of Fate, the vivid remembrance of her perfume, speaking of things exotic and forbidden. He felt from the beginning that, like the train, she was seductive and dangerous. He remembered what Piersohn had said about Hitler's vulnerability while he was traveling. A new plan took shape in his frantic brain.

This dual obsession was to haunt him during the weeks that followed—the powerful spell cast by moving trains and the search for a tall slim woman he had seen only masked. He slipped away to Nyphelheim whenever he could, risking discovery and punishment, to stand on the railroad overpass and watch the trains speed by until he was in a state of trance, or else to roam the streets—often with Trudi at his side—searching the faces of passers-by, watching the crowds that spilled out of movie houses, the Sunday strollers, the groups of shoppers and idle women taking tea in glassed-in café terraces.

One day in early March he stood on the railroad platform close to the edge, absorbing the violence and power of the trains, when, from one of the few that made local stops, a lady stepped down followed by a porter carrying two suitcases. She stood for a moment looking around for help, and Heinz stepped forward, emboldened by his state of intoxication, which made him feel magic and invisible. "May I help you find a cab, Your Royal Highness?" he said.

The woman looked sharply at the tall, fair-haired young man with red cheeks and a strange, elated expression in his gray eyes. Something in his bearing and accent were familiar but the impression was very hazy. "I think not."

"I will find you a porter," Heinz persisted.

The woman looked intrigued.

"You are trying to place me," Heinz guessed, "and you cannot. So I will give you a clue. I met you in a previous life, when you were Queen of Fate."

The woman laughed, her brown eyes sparkled, and her severe narrow face was suddenly merry. "That impossible public ball! Now, which one were you? The Spanish grandee? The polar bear? The devil? . . . But of course, my young Mephisto!" She laughed again.

Meanwhile Heinz had taken possession of her luggage and proceeded to look for a horse cab. She followed him out of the station. There was no cab in sight, so he suggested that they take tea, and if none showed up he would run and search for one. She was about to refuse, but he said, "I know it isn't proper for you to have tea with an ordinary fellow like Heinz Hauptmann"—he bowed formally—"but to dance with strange demons that appear out of the mist is all right. Isn't that what you are thinking?"

"Something like that," she admitted. "Are you Herr Hauptmann?"

"Yes. You may say to anyone who inquires that you were formally introduced to me by a demon in a red suit. So now, will you have tea?"

She sighed. She was tired and depressed, and the young man was amusing and amiable. She led the way to a table in a shabby little café across from the station—the only one in the street—and sat down gratefully. She had traveled from Berlin with two tiresome old women who talked incessantly, her worry about the future bottled up inside her while she nodded politely at their chatter. As they talked on she pondered her position, banished as she was by her Gestapo husband to a quiet little town while he worked on what were obviously secret and dangerous assignments, and it had been almost too much for her. She feared for his life, and suffered doubly because she had only recently admitted to herself that she did not love him, that her marriage had been a mistake.

Heinz looked at the name on her expensive luggage. "E. V. Enzian," he read. "The first E. is for Else. Am I right?"

"How did you know my first name?" she asked.

"Demons are clairvoyant," said Heinz with a smug smile. Else realized that he must have heard it at the ball. It was flattering to think he might have taken pains to remember it. She guessed his age at about twenty, which made him some five or six years younger than she, but masquerade balls are well known for their power to kindle romantic fancies. In her mood of disillusion with herself and her life, it was pleasant to think she might have a young admirer in the handsome youth with the Polish accent and German name. She guessed he was a *Volksdeutsche*, recently repatriated, and likely soon to be conscripted.

"Well, then, you can easily guess the rest," she challenged him. Heinz looked crestfallen. The café was chilly and grim—a place frequented by railroad crews, not the tourists who came to Nyphelheim for its pure air and mountain sports. The tea cheered her, and she became more communicative. Her home in Berlin had been destroyed, she told him, and she was staying in Nyphelheim alone, because she had relatives nearby. She said she did some volunteer work in a hospital and passed the time as best she could until it would be safe to return to Berlin.

"After the victory," said Heinz, a conditioned reflex. His mind was not working properly, what with Else's perfume and the low-cut neckline of her dress, revealed by the open coat and floating silk scarf.

She did not reply. After the victory Willi would come home to her, a conqueror, covered with decorations and rewarded with high rank. She would be one more ornament to his splendor, with no purpose in life but to do his will and reflect honor on his name. Perhaps if she had children, she would not mind the bleakness of such a life. But to conceive a child, didn't there have to be harmony between them, a oneness of the flesh? In their short marriage, she had never known such a feeling with Willi. In fact, it was clear to her that the kind of woman who aroused his desire was one for whom he could feel the greatest contempt —a paid prostitute, perhaps. Were all men like that? she wondered. The clear-eyed youth across the table from her—blushing now when she observed his eyes delicately exploring her body—surely he would be a gentle bedfellow. She wanted a lover, not a conqueror.

"There is a horse cab," said Heinz. He ran to the street to call to the driver who was delivering a family to the station. He carried out Else's bags while she collected herself and paid the waiter. Heinz was somewhat abashed, but she tucked the rug around their legs and pressed his hand gently under its cover as the driver coaxed the horse into a street leading into the center of town. Heinz could not speak, nor could he control the signs of his desire.

At the doorway to her apartment, a narrow stairs between a dry-cleaning shop and a dressmaker, she said in a carrying voice, "Don't trouble, my brother will take the bags up," and dismissed the driver. Heinz, his cheeks burning and his heart pounding, started up the steep stairs with the two valises. Else had her key ready, and he hurried into the entryway. Without a word, she took off her coat and dropped it over the luggage, then turned and stood smiling up at him, her cold hand on his chest inside his coat. He kissed her mouth tenderly, as innocent Trudi had taught him, but Else was no Trudi. She was a passionate woman driven nearly to desperation.

Very soon they were half undressed on Else's bed, she gently leading him in a ritual he had only dimly pieced together from his hasty coupling with Basia in the barn loft when he was fourteen and the bawdy conversations of his schoolmates, reinforced by the erotic dreams he entertained of future conquests and delights. She guided him into her body and whispered, "Wait for me." He could not wait long, but her whimpering and the strong grasp of her thighs told him he need not. When they drew apart, he saw tears were streaming from her eyes and she was sobbing quietly against him.

"Why are you sad?" he asked her. "Are you sorry for what we did?"

Else shook her head no, and bit his shoulder where her mouth lay against him. "I am crying for happiness," she murmured.

Heinz did not believe her, but he was not in a mood to press for the truth. Idly he took off the rest of her clothes and looked at her with wonder, his desire growing as he explored her soft body. She taught him then how to arouse her a second time and a third, and they spent the afternoon in a spinning vortex of sensuality, from which it became more and more difficult to break away to the real world they had left behind. At last, spent, Heinz dozed off, still entwined about her body. He slept until she woke him with hot coffee. She was bathed and wrapped in a soft flannel robe. "Breakfast time," she nudged him. While they restored themselves, she explained to him seriously that they could meet again, but not without difficulty. She did not want to be compromised, but she would think of some plan. Heinz could not believe his luck. He hated confessing that he was a student at the high school and was free only on Sunday afternoons.

"And you surely have a sweetheart," she teased him. "But she does not treat you as well as I do?"

Heinz blushed, and said he would try to think of a plan too. Trudi and their afternoon walks were very far from his mind. He would find a way to get out of the school on other days—bribe the gatekeeper, get a friend to cover up for him. When Heinz left Else that morning, the sun was red in the sky, and as he descended the wooden staircase that led from her apartment, in the distance he heard the mournful whistle of a train through the fresh morning air.

Over the next several weeks they met wherever and whenever

they could. They made love in the mountain forest and, when they could arrange it, in her warm bed. It was several weeks before Heinz discovered that she was married. He was stunned and angry.

"Frau Bismar," he heard the owner of the dry-cleaning shop call her one day as he waited outside her apartment.

"So you are Frau Bismar?" he challenged her when she came back in, carrying the key to the shop. It was closed on a Sunday, but she wanted to go in and pick up a dress to wear that evening.

"Does it make a difference to you?"

"Are you a widow, Frau Bismar?" Heinz asked. Then he said suddenly, "Never mind. I don't want to know." He was not what he seemed, so why should he fault others for deception? But he felt defrauded, ill-used.

Else was in a black mood, as she was more and more often now. "I am not a widow. I am an adulteress. Is that what you wanted to hear?"

"For me you were the Queen of Fate," said Heinz. "Fate is a dangerous mistress." But her anger would not be stilled.

"How cynical you have grown," said Else. She drew his face down to hers. "Because I kept you waiting. Because I put you off last week. Because you are impatient."

"Your husband is at the front," said Heinz bitterly. He thought of the Germans streaming into Polansk; the "front" was terrified villagers, men lined up and shot and piled in a trench.

"Yes, on and off." Else was weary to death with thinking that very thought. The front. The Russians. Willi's victorious return. Willi killed by the Bolsheviks or the partisans. "He is an officer of the *Reichssicherheitsdienst*, a special unit of the SS. Now are you satisfied?" Her voice was sharp and cruel, as he had never heard it before. She wanted to hurt herself as well as Heinz, but he could not guess as much. He took hold of her arm to turn her around. He wanted to silence her, punish her. See what her eyes held for him behind the words—hatred, revenge, contempt? His abrupt gesture startled her. She retreated from him. He pursued her and, with a violence unlike any he had ever known, forced her down on the bed.

She gasped as he took her savagely, not waiting for her pleasure, no longer cajoling and caressing as she had taught him. It was as though, at the mention of Willi, his corrupt spirit had poisoned her young and gentle lover. Heinz was sweating, raging, weeping, as he raped his struggling victim. A painful memory of the churchyard where his father died, and where he had given up his name, overtook him. "Died during the interrogation" was the phrase that Father Sebastian had used to describe his mother's death, and he found himself repeating this lowly to himself as he exploded with a shudder in the Nazi woman.

When Heinz recovered from his trembling and nausea, Else was gone. The door was ajar, and he slipped out, pulling it locked behind him. He was weak with rage as he made his way back to the Oberschule. Weak with rage, but strong with resolve. Hitler would die.

As the weeks passed and Else disappeared from his life, Heinz regretted his rash action. He needed her and wanted her back—her dark beauty, her sensuality. Perhaps he did not love her, but he desired her painfully. He took to wandering in the forest above the Oberschule where they had met, watching the wild flowers blossom along the paths they had followed. He climbed the rock face of the Great Sampson, sometimes looking down into the abyss below him with irony, tempting his evil genius to push him to his death.

One such day, as he returned from his climb, he found Else waiting for him at their trysting place. She was more beautiful than he remembered. She held out her hand and he let her lead him through the thicket to a small clearing. Without a word, she began their familiar play, drawing him to her, locking him into her darkness until they both burst free. She sat up and caressed his face. "You see, I have forgiven you. Have you forgiven me?" She understood his pain, the disillusionment of youth. He had not forgiven her, but he desired her more than ever. In reply, he kissed her.

Else talked to him about her failed marriage, her fear of the future. Her husband no longer loomed as a sexual rival, although Heinz knew that the risk they ran was very great. A domestic scandal could ruin an SS officer's career, and his revenge would no doubt be brutal. Neither Heinz nor Else, fully aware of this, could focus on reality. The risks they ran every day—in the street, in cafés, at home, in shops and churches—were mounting daily, as though in counterpoint to the risks of battle. Else's talk of Willi became compulsive, as though she could exorcise the threat of his return by a ritual evocation for his violence. Heinz saw the sadness in her eyes, and was sorry for his violence.

Toward the end of the term, a series of disquieting events took place. First, Andreas told him that Herr Piersohn was in Nyphelheim; he had come without warning, and Andreas had met him only by chance. He was planning to visit the school and call on his young friends, of course, he told Andreas, but he had business to attend to first. Then Else pointed him out to Heinz as they ducked around a corner to avoid him, asking, "Have you seen that man before?"

"Yes," Heinz replied. "I know him slightly." He had told her briefly about his summer in Munich, and identified Piersohn as the eccentric old fairy who had showed so much interest in him and his friend Andreas. They had laughed over it together, but now Else became serious.

"Stay away from him," she said. "I have no real proof, but I know he has some connection with the Gestapo. He is dangerous, Heinz."

Heinz, who understood the extent of his danger better than she could possibly guess, could only nod. Later the same day, he saw Piersohn deep in conversation with Dr. Neufeind at the back of a shabby café. Then Else sent him a message, through Andreas. As he opened the letter, which was sealed with a pale red wax, his eyes fell on the bad news that Herr Bismar was home on furlough.

The news cast Heinz into a deep depression. He had been used to the idea that Else was his; the thought of the black Gestapo uniform in the room where he and Else had made love filled him with despair. But as deep as his sense of loss was, it would not overcome him. His plan was already in motion.

Heinz began to feel lonely and rejected. He longed for his homeland. He desired to return to Poland, now called General Gouvernement. He wanted to speak his native language again, to see the fields and trees of his native country.

The knowledge that this might be his last chance to visit his native land strengthened this desire. Heinz was expected to be drafted within a few weeks or months. Germany was fighting an offensive war on an extended front in Russia. In Africa the Germans had occupied Tobruk and crossed the Egyptian border. All these victories cost hundreds of thousands dead and wounded who had to be replaced. The students in the Oberschule, who in the first two years of the war had been allowed to finish the school before being drafted, were now being called to service. In Heinz's class, seven boys had been inducted into various branches of German military forces since the beginning of the school year.

Heinz and the other students who had not been drafted were expected to spend six weeks of their vacation in an SS summer training camp. In this way the SS could recruit the best students for service with them. The camp was located on a Bavarian farm and participants were trained in horsemanship and other sports. At the end there would be pressure to sign up with the SS.

Heinz did not want to spend six weeks with the SS and managed eventually to be excused. He claimed a need to put his estate in order before being drafted. He had to fill in countless forms, which had to be approved and stamped. Eventually he obtained the necessary travel documents.

When Heinz's trip was approved, he began to think also about his first girl friend, Lilka. He wondered where she was and longed to see her again.

Heinz decided to accept an invitation pressed on him earlier by the other Volksdeutsche from Poland in his class, Heinrich Stroebe, to spend the summer with him in Cracow. It meant disregarding Father Sebastian's warning to stay out of Poland—but now Munich, Salzburg, Rabenden, and Nyphelheim all seemed to hold equal dangers for him. He had another reason for wanting to visit Poland's ancient capital city: he knew a doctor there, one Stephan Krzesniak, who had been a friend of Lilka's father. His own mother had often cited the name, in the course of family quarrels over how to treat an earache or summer cold, as the ultimate medical authority. Heinz hoped he might find the man and so get news of Lilka Konarski and her family.

Heinrich was proud to have his invitation accepted by the school's best athlete, a boy, moreover, whose prestige was not inconsiderably heightened by rumors of his sexual exploits.

XIII

June 1942

Obersturmbannführer Rudolf Malec of the SS sat in his office in Berlin waiting for his three closest associates to appear. Of the men under his direct command, young SS Obersturmführer Dietrich Rüger, the lowest in rank, was the only one who had his personal sympathy. Malec openly disliked SS Sturmbannführer Cart and would have had him transferred to another section had he not been indispensable. Friedrich Cart was punctilious, pedantic, and totally dedicated. He also had an uncanny and sometimes convenient resemblance to the Führer. His most studious daily occupation was brushing his uniform; he also took great pleasure in shining his boots. He loved the order and ceremony of Gestapo life, even in its smallest routines. He had no family, and spent as much of his time as he could in his office. Even at home, he wore his black uniform. Malec doubted whether he owned any other attire.

Pondering it, Malec concluded that Cart was the closest thing to a man without a soul. He was a mannequin, and indeed if he had a capacity for love, he reserved that love for his SS uniform, his pistol, and all the visible trappings of his rank. Malec doubted that Cart revered the Führer. He certainly had no feeling for his own kinsmen. He had recently filed a memorandum renouncing any connection with his brother, a Catholic priest who had received a warning from the Gestapo.

Rudolf Malec did not care for Hauptsturmführer Wilhelm Bismar either. The red-headed youth came well recommended. His family were wealthy industrialists from Krefeld; their fortune dated back to the last century, and it rankled Malec to encounter a man on whom privilege had been bestowed so blindly while he had had to struggle for every step forward out of poverty and obscurity. Malec could not forgive him his good fortune or his quick wit and elegant manner. He was well aware, too, that Bismar's whole appearance masked ugly instincts. The Gestapo informer system put revealing information in Malec's hands and he was familiar with the minutest details of Bismar's life. He knew of his marital problems, of his extramarital affairs, of a personal cruelty and vindictiveness that dated to childhood.

Sometimes Malec wondered why Bismar had joined the Gestapo. He had repeatedly demonstrated that he failed to share Malec's respect for National Socialism. In fact, Malec was sure Bismar believed in little outside himself and the efficacy of his own superiority.

Cart and Bismar arrived punctually at ten-thirty.

Malec saluted them formally and kept them standing. He looked from one to the other in distaste, but said nothing. Bismar remained perfectly correct, but one sandy eyebrow raised a fraction of an inch was enough to communicate his distaste and to infuriate his superior. Cart stood at attention, sublime in his military splendor. Faced with the two, Malec sank into his chair with a small explosion of exasperation. "At ease, gentlemen," he said. "Please be seated."

Bismar raised the other eyebrow perceptibly, a query. "Feel free to smoke," Malec added. At that point Rüger came in at a run, panted out "Heil Hitler!" and clicked his heels together. Cart ostentatiously checked his watch to emphasize that Rüger was five minutes late. But Malec smiled at the young man and gestured him to a chair.

"You have the report?" he asked Rüger and Rüger extracted a thick envelope from an inside pocket and handed it over. Cart and Bismar exchanged glances, but Malec only laid the mysterious package on his desk, tapping it idly with his fingertips while he talked.

"I have called this meeting to discuss special arrangements for the Führer's protection during his trip from Wolfsschanze to Berlin and Berchtesgaden," he said. "We still have not been able to identify Komm's group. We found the name and address of Boleslaw Leski among his effects, but, beyond that, our investigation has come to nothing."

"When a member of the NASDP in good standing commits suicide rather than answer routine questions, it is fairly suggestive," said Bismar. He put a cigarette in his holder but did not light it. "It suggests that the danger may originate high up in the Party, which may be why none of our tactics have flushed them."

"They have every advantage," said Malec, tapping on the envelope. Cart crossed his knees and contemplated the light reflecting off his boot. They had been over this ground before. He knew Malec was stalling them just to indulge in his self-importance. But he would eventually have to tell them what was in the envelope, or forfeit his whole effect.

Bismar lighted his cigarette and blew a cloud of smoke upward. Only Rüger, who gazed at the Obersturmbannführer with a look of expectation and awe, was responsive to Malec's attempt to dramatize the situation. "What I have here," Malec finally began, "are the scraps of the original and reconstruction of parts of Komm's notebook. You will recall that it was partially destroyed and largely illegible."

At last all three officers were listening intently.

"Our decoding division has submitted a plausible version." He tapped the envelope. "It connects Komm with a plot which we believe was the Elser bombing. Certain details date it about the same time, and they imply that Komm's group was to explode a poison gas bomb independently in case Elser failed."

"Elser did not know about them, presumably," Cart pointed out.

"Those papers that Komm took to Poland, they are the key," said Malec. "There we are at a standstill. The Leski estate has been leveled, the house virtually taken apart stone by stone. We have dug through thousands of cubic meters of earth looking for those papers. You, Captain Cart, were present at Frau Leski's interrogation."

"We were all present at Leski's execution," said Cart softly, admiring his other boot. Malec grew purple in the face. One of the major mistakes of his career, he told himself angrily, was letting their star witnesses be killed before their eyes.

"The Führer is going to travel within the next few months," he said loudly. "This group is undetected and is capable of another attempt on the Führer's life."

Bismar raised his hand and his eyebrow asking for the floor. Malec nodded sullenly. Bismar rose and began pacing the room importantly, like a general planning battle strategy, Malec realized.

"Our enemy is important, highly placed," Bismar started. He ticked off his index finger. "He must be well-informed. He has antennae in sundry places—for example, headquarters of the Gestapo in major cities." He ticked off his middle finger. "He therefore must employ agents." He looked up, holding his left ring finger between the thumb and index of his right hand. "These agents do not know each other."

The room was silent. He went on, "One of them must be vulnerable. Or at least one must have doubts, hesitation; or else have something to gain by selling information. Suppose just one of these agents could be bought. It might help."

"How do you mean, bought? What are you planning to offer?" asked Cart.

"I suppose there are persons of good standing in our Party who have secrets—skeletons in their closet?" He looked around the room. Each man knew what he meant. "Some may want a colleague with an embarrassing memory erased; some might want a Jew's life saved, a prisoner allowed to escape and escorted out of the country—that kind of thing."

"We spread a rumor," Bismar went on, pacing more slowly. "Very delicately. In a very few places—Gestapo headquarters in Berlin, Munich, General Gouvernement, Salzburg. News like that will spread fast. We mention Komm, some missing papers, perhaps Leski—no more. The person who has the information knows what we want better than we do."

"Komm may be the only one who knew about Leski," objected Cart. "Of course we would buy the information that Komm gave the papers to Leski—but anyone who has such knowledge may know more. Let him first come forward—then we can bargain."

Malec turned his back to the room and looked out the window. The plan was clever, and Bismar was no doubt the best man for the job. But it rankled him that Bismar had come up with it. "Lieutenant Bismar, you've talked yourself into a job," he said, in an attempt at joviality. "You can start immediately. I want a copy of your itinerary, and a daily report by telephone." With a gesture he indicated that the others were dismissed. They saluted and left.

XIV

July 1942

The boys took a horse cab from the station. Heinrich said he always did, which sounded to Heinz pretentious and fabricated, although it could easily have been true. The Stroebes lived in an old house in the best section of town, which was now reserved for Germans. Tall windows and a circular staircase with marble steps showed that it had once been an elegant town house. Now a rickety elevator was fitted into the one corner behind the stairs, and the floors were divided into apartments. The boys went up to the third floor, where the Stroebes lived in a large apartment that was newly furnished with imitation French antiques. Herr Stroebe was *Treuhänder* in a sausage factory, which, while it remained in the hands of its Polish owners, had to have a German manager to represent the Fatherland's interests. Herr Stroebe had been recruited from his own flourishing butcher shop in Tarnopol to serve as factory manager, and among the many benefits of his new position, one he took most advantage of was access to a lucrative black market.

His Louis XVI chairs and crystal chandelier bore witness to his business sense and acumen. He wore shoes of crocodile skin and a large gold ring set with a ruby. Heinz was more impressed by his size than his wealth. Over six feet tall and extremely fat, he filled space ceremoniously, like some huge rhinoceros. He greeted Heinz in a heavily accented German, made a few formal remarks, like a welcoming committee, then sighed heavily and lapsed into Polish. He seldom spoke German again—it was only with the arrival of the Nazis that he had begun to value his superior cultural heritage; as a local butcher in a Polish town he had never given it much thought. Like the tiny gilded chairs he could not sit on, the blood of the superrace in his veins was an encumbrance and a superfluous ornament. In the company of the delicate brocaded pieces was a large plush armchair for the master of the house; there he sat enthroned and viewed his unexpected splendor. A Jewish family had been removed from the apartment to make room for the Stroebes; they now lived in the ghetto, which was more seemly in the newly ordered society.

Heinrich's mother was a large-boned, colorless woman, as tall as her husband, silent and melancholy except when she was fussing over Heinrich, her only child and, it appeared, her life's one delight. None of her husband's luxurious possessions seemed to impress her; she obediently polished and dusted them and kept them in order, as she had kept the humble belongings of her small house in back of the butcher shop in Tarnopol.

Heinz felt a certain sympathy for these people, so ill at ease in their own lives, without quite knowing why. They were certainly glad to be German in times like these when Poles were shunted about like cattle, made to live in the shabby sections of the city, ride in third-class railroad cars and trams, and were barred from the best theaters and movie houses. They often marveled at their luck; it was like having inherited money from a distant relative they never knew existed.

Heinz and Heinrich were stuffed with food punctually four times a day, and after the meager, poorly cooked meals at school, both ate voraciously. The Stroebes had a Polish cook who made wonderful beet soup with *uszki*—little pastry "ears" stuffed with meat—and typical strips of fried pastry, and of course there was never a lack of good Cracow sausage.

The boys went strolling through the city; Heinrich was almost as much a stranger there as Heinz. They dutifully inspected the old market square and the ancient churches and explored the Wawel castle and browsed about its monuments. Heinrich was a phlegmatic companion, silent except for the official speeches he would sometimes deliver in honor of some historical site or event of note, in the manner of a village mayor at a public function. Heinz could not make him out. He completely lacked a sense of humor and was puritanical in his attitude toward girls. He openly disapproved of the flirtatious, pretty ones in tight sweaters who caught Heinz's eye as they passed. His one passion was building model ships, and Heinz finally left him to it and went out into the city on his own.

He was careful to wear the insignia of the Hitler Youth in his lapel—he did not particularly want to have his papers inspected or his identity scrutinized. The emblem did not make him welcome in Polish shops or gathering places. He could sense the hostility of the people, even waiting for a trolley on a street corner. The insignia meant he had privileges; he would not be taken in a random roundup of young men to be shipped off arbitrarily for farm labor in Germany; he did not have to observe the humiliating curfew which kept Poles off the streets after dark. Here in the city that was his country's jewel, miraculously preserved from war's insults, he was treated as a stranger and an enemy.

One day as he was making his way through the old section of town, near St. Florian's Gate, he came upon the office of a Dr. Krzesniak. It was in a small, old building, marked with a white enamel plaque bearing the doctor's name in black letters and announcing his specialty: *internista*. Heinz could not decide what to do. The doctor would not know him by sight, yet he felt he must hide until he had worked out a plan. He stood in a doorway down the street watching the entrance half the afternoon, but no one resembling Dr. Krzesniak appeared—in fact no one seemed to go in or out except old women with kerchiefs over their heads. Finally it was time to go back to the Stroebes' laden tea table, with its dark moist breads and babkas and delicate jam of wood strawberries.

The next morning, Heinz went boldly to the house and asked the porter for Dr. Krzesniak. The old man was sweeping the stairs, and took his time before replying. "Second floor. He'll be in about noon." He gave a cool, respectful look at the Hitler Youth button on Heinz's collar. "Are you a patient?"

"No. A friend," said Heinz.

The old man made a contemptuous sound, then, to ward off evil spirits, spat over his shoulder. "Friend," he said neutrally, as though the word meant "stone" or "yesterday."

"A friend of a friend," Heinz corrected. "I'll come back. Good day," he added, and made a quick exit. He could feel the old man staring at his back.

He made his way to the Czartoryski palace, but he hardly saw where he was going, since he was intensely preoccupied with the thought of how it would feel to say "I am Adam Leski." Each time he tried to imagine himself standing in front of the doctor, announcing his name, he trembled with excitement and dread. Adam Leski was shot by the Germans as a hostage. His body was buried with eleven others in a common grave in Poland. Thinking about it, Heinz could feel the gooseflesh on his forearms.

When it was a quarter to twelve, he set out for the doctor's office. Before he went into the house, he took off the Hitler Youth emblem and put it in his pocket. A naked bulb burned behind a white-curtained window on the second floor; Heinz marked it out as the doctor's examining room. He went bravely up the stairs and rang the bell. An old woman in a black dress opened the door and stood barring the way without a word.

"Dr. Krzesniak, if you please," said Heinz politely.

"Do you have an appointment?" The women did not budge.

"Tell him, please, that a friend of Dr. Jan Konarski's, from Katowice, is here. A friend of his daughter's."

The woman closed the door and left Heinz on the landing. After a moment she returned and let him in without speaking.

He entered a dark little waiting room and stood uncertainly beside a table. He felt he was being observed, although no one was in sight.

Finally the doctor came to the door and bowed slightly. "Young man, you say that you knew Dr. Konarski? Why have you come to me?" Dr. Krzesniak was tall and thin, bearded and bespectacled. His hands looked transparent, and blue veins showed on his temples and forehead.

"Yes, sir. I was a school friend of Lilka and Wacek's. And a pupil of Pani Doktorowa's. Before the war. I want to find them if I can."

"Well, you can't, and you must leave here," said the doctor curtly. He turned to leave the room.

"Please, Dr. Krzesniak," Heinz pleaded. "Why do you say that? Why can't I find them?"

The doctor turned back. "Aren't you the German boy who was observing this house and came asking for me this morning?" he asked. "What do you want with your Jewish friends now?"

"Dr. Krzesniak, I am a Pole. My name is . . ." He swallowed. "I can explain, but it is very complicated. I want to find Lilka and her family because . . . I might help them. My parents were killed by the Germans at the beginning of the war. I have no one left."

The doctor stood in silence, watching him during this rush of words and confused emotions. Of course the doctor had no way of knowing whether he was lying, Heinz realized. A German boy had been looking for the doctor; the city was full of informers. The old janitor had probably seen him watching the house the day before. "I have German papers. I am hiding in Germany." Impulsively, he plunged in. "My father was Boleslaw Leski, a landowner in Polansk." Heinz was out of breath, as though he had been running or climbing a hill. If the doctor wanted to, he could turn him over to the Gestapo. But instead he came over to him and took him by the shoulder.

"Come into the examining room," he said, leading the way. "Boleslaw Leski," he said in a low voice. "How do I know you are telling the truth?"

"Did you know my father?" asked Heinz.

"In a way," said the doctor. "Who sent you here?"

"I came on my own. I'm trying to find Lilka and her family."

"Nothing more than that?"

"What more is there?" asked Heinz. "No." This doctor was a strange man. His bluish fingers were shaking, his piercing black eyes, magnified through the thick lenses, probed like surgical instruments.

"Tell me, if you are Boleslaw Leski's son, where is Father Sebastian?"

"You know Father Sebastian?" asked Heinz in astonishment.

"Do you?" asked the doctor. But Heinz had passed the test.

"He was my tutor. He saved my life. He came to me in Germany and told me the Gestapo tortured my mother and killed her." His voice was toneless, as if the words meant nothing. "I never saw him after that."

"All right," said Dr. Krzesniak and clapped his hands on his knees. "I'll tell you this much. Dr. Konarski is dead. The Germans shot him as a hostage some months back. Magda and the children were here in Cracow. After Jan was killed they moved to Czestochowa. They would be living somewhere in the ghetto. It is not a very big city. I'll give you the name of a colleague who might help you find them. But what can you do for them, young man? Tell me that? How will you defend them against this terror? I could not help them, and I am considerably older and more experienced than you."

"I want to see them. I don't know whether I could do anything or not. I want to say good-bye." As he said it Heinz realized for the first time what he had come to Poland for.

"Here is the name of a doctor in Czestochowa," said Dr. Krzesniak, writing a name on his prescription pad. "You'd better not come back here. I am watched."

Heinz could not find his voice to say thank you. He took one cold blue hand in his to say good-bye and nodded emphatically. He knew he would burst into tears if he spoke.

As he went through the hall, he passed the old janitor and nodded briskly. As soon as he rounded the corner, he put his Hitler

Youth emblem back on his lapel. In a doorway he took out the prescription sheet on which the doctor had written the name of his friend: Dr. Henryk Bronsztajn. On the way back to the Stroebes' apartment, he tore it up, rolled the pieces into tiny balls, and dropped them into drains and flower pots and trash cans along his way.

The only train to Czestochowa left Cracow shortly before midnight and got in at two-thirty in the morning. Heinz explained to Heinrich's parents that he wanted to visit more of Poland before the summer vacation ended. He was so obviously bored with Heinrich, and Heinrich with him, that his departure came as no surprise. The family ate a farewell feast in his honor. Frau Stroebe then packed him a copious meal of bread and sausage and pickles, with a large piece of cake and a bottle of wine. He was glad to have it and thanked her sincerely. It was probably the last time he would eat that well for many months, he reflected.

He took a horse cab to the station, leaving before dark because of the curfew. As a German, he could be out as late as he liked, but Polish drivers had to be off the streets, so there were no cabs to be found once the sun went down.

Heinz boarded the train two hours before its scheduled departure. He had decided to travel with the Poles in the crowded, shabby third-class car. When Heinz came aboard, the train was already overcrowded and he had to stand leaning against a lavatory door. His fellow travelers did not fare any better. They were huddled into every corner of the train, most of them standing or leaning as best they could, many of them clutching large bundles as though they held treasures. They doubtless were carrying merchandise for sale or food from the country for the black market; for many people trading in small items acquired by craft or wit was the only way to survive the war.

The train was delayed by crowds of people struggling to get on the train but at last it was impossible to accommodate any more. Finally, the whistle signaled the train to start.

The movement of the train, with frequent jerks and sudden stops, make the trip almost unbearable. Passengers' tempers flared. An old woman was scolding two sprawling youths for taking too much space, and they were teasing her good-naturedly. A child woke up and screamed endlessly, until its distracted mother threatened, "Do you want Hitler to come and get you?" upon which it fell silent. These people scrambling for a livelihood were not unlike the villagers and peasants Heinz had known as a child; war had not made them any the less contentious or long-suffering or compassionate. He had come to say good-bye to them, silent and wary, inviting their suspicion but drawn to them by memories and deep ties of blood.

The train drew into Czestochowa while it was still dark. Passengers with German papers left the station, but the Poles, subject to the curfew, had to stay off the streets until it was light. Heinz settled himself and his suitcase against a pillar, and prepared to wait. People were milling about making plans, bartering goods, exchanging news. Some sat silent, guarding their bundles, too exhausted or too dejected to take part. Some, the solitary ones, were strangers like himself, he supposed, or possibly informers, absorbing the conversations around them.

"My cousin says the ghettos in Otwock are being liquidated," he overheard a man whisper.

"Who will be next?" a woman sighed.

"I have enough troubles of my own without worrying about the Jews," their companion rejoined. "Let them look out for themselves."

Heinz heard the sound of a locomotive. Another train arrived. The doors opened and two military policemen armed with submachine guns ordered the crowd to clear a passage. A few minutes later the first wounded soldiers were carried through the waiting room of the station to the ambulance trucks. These were followed by hundreds of wounded, many missing legs or arms.

They had had to make a long train journey from the front several hundred kilometers away. They had fought near Stalingrad, Voronesh, or Maikop. It had taken them days to reach Czestochowa and a hospital. Here, in the occupied enemy country, they would be treated and operated upon. Those who survived, but were unable to fight again, would return home. They would travel in small groups. A trainful of wounded would have a bad impact in their Fatherland. Others, who would recover, would rejoin their units on the Don or near the Volga to continue their war.

Heinz thought he might meet one of his former colleagues from the Oberschule among these wounded soldiers, but he did not recognize anyone. Will he one day be carried on a stretcher? he thought.

"Our time will come, mark my words," the first voice, frail and petulant, went on.

"Will the Jews help you out then?" asked the other man. He spat in contempt.

We must all look out for each other, Heinz thought. He glimpsed the silhouette of an armed guard against the pale light outside the station. These people waiting inside for the dawn to release them believed that, if they were patient and subservient, they would be overlooked; others would stand in meadows facing the Nazi firing squads, and after the war others would bring flowers to decorate the place. A spectacle he would not live to witness, he reflected. If he succeeded in his plan, he would have avenged both the living and the dead.

Finally the dim brown light turned to silvery gray and the passengers began to leave the station. They hurried on their ways, dispersing into the city streets. Heinz followed a family group of several children with their parents, all lugging heavy suitcases, and asked the way to the shrine of the Virgin in the Church of Jasna Gora. As a child he had been taken with his first Communion class to visit the chapel with the miraculous image. Even the Nazi conquerors had not dared to prevent the people of Poland from visiting their Madonna to pray for their country's deliverance.

"You cross that square and turn right, you'll see the Aleja Najswietszej Marii Panny," the woman answered his inquiry. "You can see the monastery at the far end."

"Adolf Hitler Allee," a boy of about twelve corrected her.

"Keep your mouth shut. I know what I mean," said his mother, slapping his face smartly. "Adolf Hitler Allee!" She spat on the pavement.

"Thank you, *dziekuje Pani*," said Heinz and headed quickly

across the square before he could cause any more family strife. He followed the long avenue that used to bear the name of the Most Blessed Virgin up to the holy place on the hill, where the miraculous image had chosen of its own will to stay forever, according to the legend which was more beloved than believed by its fervent petitioners. He entered the church and found a mass in progress at the main altar. It was a moment before he realized he had happened on a funeral mass. He stood respectfully while the priest circled the bier, swinging the gold censer and praying for the remission of sins and the soul's repose in everlasting light. The sweetness and safety of death held him rapt for an instant, then he fought off the delusion and went toward the chapel that held the Madonna of Czestochowa, a powerful intercessor and protectress whose favor he devoutly desired. Childhood prayers and childhood memories overpowered him. "Hail, Mary full of grace," his mind reiterated as he stood before the shrine. "Pray for us sinners now and at the hour of our death." He could think of nothing more to ask, for himself or for those he loved, than what men had been praying for down all the ages. It would be enough.

On the way out, he bought a wallet-sized picture of the Madonna. He made his way back down the wide avenue planted with tall poplars; it would soon be a decent hour to attempt to find Dr. Bronsztajn.

He entered the ghetto, still following the central avenue; side streets were already filled with people coming and going, packing and unpacking bundles, stopping to talk and hurrying on as though to urgent appointments. Everyone wore the Star of David on his armband; SS troops patrolled in pairs, and the streets emptied before them as they passed. There were now almost daily roundups of Jews for deportation to resettlement centers; rumor said they were never resettled, but taken to prison camps and shot. No one could either confirm or deny it, and whatever the truth was, most people felt it was futile to fight an implacable destiny. The fate of partisans and resisters at least was clear; the public hangings and shootings left nothing to rumor.

Heinz entered a busy street and approached an old man sitting in front of a little bookstall; both looked as if they had been there for hundreds of years. He asked how he might find a certain Dr. Henryk Bronsztajn, and the old man nodded knowingly. He said something in Yiddish to a woman who sat knitting in the shadow in the alleyway behind the bookstall. She shook her head and murmured a reply.

"Dr. Bronsztajn has been resettled in the new territory. He has emigrated. He will not be back." Tears stood in the old man's eyes. The woman said something sharp and no doubt critical for he quickly changed his position and straightened his spine.

"You are his friend?" asked Heinz. "Did you know him?"

The old man did not answer. It was not wise to tell a stranger who one's friends were. Heinz should know that.

"I thought he could help me find my friends here in Czestochowa. They came from Cracow. Their name is Konarski. Lilka and Wacek . . . so if you hear where they are, tell them . . ." Heinz hesitated. "Tell them a schoolmate of theirs is here. A pupil of Pani Doktorowa. Tell them Dr. Krzesniak in Cracow . . ."

The woman's voice interrupted him, speaking rapidly to the man.

"My wife says they went to Warsaw. When Henryk, when Dr. Bronsztajn . . . emigrated."

"Warsaw!" exclaimed Heinz. "How will I ever find them there?" The old man shrugged his shoulders and spread out his hands, palms up. The woman bobbed her head from side to side, indicating that it was none of their affair, and one should not expect miracles in this life.

Heinz realized that the conversation was at an end and thanked the old couple politely. The station was only a few blocks away, but he could not bring himself to return to it and take a train to Warsaw without trying to get more information. He knew that Lilka's mother was originally from Warsaw; there had been a grandmother who sent wonderful toys to the children and who insisted that Lilka go to finishing school in the capital so that she would have fine manners and know how to behave in society. But how was he to find them? He decided to try to find someone else who knew Dr. Bronsztajn—someone more communicative. He went into three pharmacies, and asked the way to the railroad station from dour and monosyllabic clerks, until he found a pleasant, round-faced woman in attendance. He asked her whether it was true that Dr. Henryk Bronsztajn had been deported, as he had heard from the old bookseller.

The woman said she did not know, but that he could easily find out by inquiring at the Franke House, where the doctor had his office. It was a big fine-looking building on the Adolf Hitler Allee, near the railroad.

The house was guarded by a white-haired porter with the arrogant bearing of one who has seen service in the best of houses. He confirmed the bookseller's story, adding that the Agrest family had indeed gone on to Warsaw to join their relatives there.

Agrest. Heinz remembered now. Grandmother Agrest. The pride, the reputation, the wealth of the Agrests. Pani Doktorowa Konarski had resumed her maiden name, no doubt to cast her lot unequivocally with her people, in defiance of the Führer's madness. Lilka and Wacek would have followed her example. That night Heinz took a train to Warsaw, his apprehension growing. Perhaps the once influential and wealthy Agrests would have found a way to fend off the terror—he had heard people talk of false papers, hiding places, even escape routes out of the country, all to be had for a price—but his instinct told him that the Konarskis had not gone to Warsaw to look for a way to save themselves.

His train reached the city in the early morning. Warsaw looked busy, immense, intent on its own affairs. In spite of the piles of rubble that once had been imposing buildings, the bullet-pocked walls, the patrols of black-uniformed SS men, the city carried on its complicated round of ceremonies and intrigues and struggles; crippled, disgraced, enraged, it was still strident with life. To find one family—especially one that might be in hiding—seemed a hopeless task. He roamed the streets, finally ending up in a café on Aleja Marszalkowska. He struck up a conversation with a morose-looking young man who told him he worked in a bakery nights, so had his days free. He was waiting for his sweetheart, who worked as a maid in a German household, to come out to do the morning marketing. Heinz said he was a high school student, and the boy remarked that it was unhealthy for Poles to be anything but laborers. "When they finish off the Jews, we'll be next," he explained. "The only Jews they aren't taking are the factory workers. You'd better learn a trade and forget about high school," he advised, "because we'll be next."

"What do you mean 'taking'? Where are they taking them?"

The youth shrugged his shoulders. "Labor camps, resettlement centers. They resettle them in the next world, if you ask me. They just ship them out by the hundreds, load them into freight cars, and that's the last of them. Half the ghetto must be empty by now."

"But where to? Where do the trains go?"

"What do you care? Wherever they take them, they don't come back. Some people say they shoot them, some say they gas them with poison. They shot my brother, right in front of the post office, with a bunch of other university students. That was in '39." With that the boy seemed to lose interest in the conversation and went back to toying with his glass.

Heinz decided to take a chance. "My parents were killed in '39 too," he said. "Now I'm looking for a family I used to know." He paused. "A Jewish family."

The youth looked at him in alarm. "The ghetto is closed. You can't go there. Unless you can sneak in some way. It's dangerous. Even more dangerous for them to sneak out. Do you know where they live?"

"No," Heinz admitted.

"I advise you to forget it, then. You know what happens to Poles who help Jews?" He drew his finger across his neck. A pretty girl of about seventeen came and sat down next to them.

"I can't stay," she said, glancing suspiciously at Heinz. "Come with me while I buy bread. I've got extra coupons."

The young man got up slowly; he was clearly exhausted. He gestured a brief farewell to Heinz. They had gone a few steps, whispering to each other, when the girl came back to his table, alighting like a bird about to fly off again. "If you go to the district court in Leszno, you can go in from the Aryan side. It is inside the ghetto, and Jews come there to sell things. Lawyers, too, from the ghetto. You might find someone to help you." She smiled at him and waved. "Good luck."

In his surprise, Heinz had almost failed to pay attention to the directions. She was bright and trim and pretty—nothing like the maids he had known in Polansk before the war. Leszno, the district court—it was worth a try.

He found the court building, a large dignified structure whose corridors had been turned into a kind of bazaar, swirling with confusion. After confiding in several people that he was looking for a family named Agrest, and meeting with incredulous or uncomprehending stares, he finally found a peddler of gold rings who said, "Wait outside that door. Mecenas Agrest is following a case. He will come out sooner or later. He is very tall, with a black beard. Ask him." The man folded up his case and disappeared.

Heinz posted himself where he could see the door, and when two black-bearded men emerged, talking with animated gestures, he approached the taller one. Stumbling over his words, he told the forbidding stranger his mission, the revelations of Dr. Krzesniak and the disappearance of Dr. Bronsztajn. The man stared at him in amazement. "Lilka and Wacek Konarski?" he finally queried. Heinz nodded. "You could give them a message, you don't have to tell me where they are. Tell them, tell Pani Doktorowa, just say that a friend from Polansk came to greek them."

"Just what is your connection with the Konarskis?" the lawyer started. Heinz was beginning to despair of getting any help when the man suddenly seemed to lose interest and at the same time to hunch forward and shrink in size. "My dear young fellow, there is no sense trying to put a good face on our misfortunes. All Jews are doomed. My cousin Magda just happened to be among the first. They came to Warsaw knowing the danger. Magda, Pani Doktorowa Konarski, was taken away along with the patients when she was visiting her mother in the hospital. Lilka, your young friend, is working in an orphanage in Mydzieszyn. Even now the SS are circling those suburban ghettos like vultures over a corpse. It is only a matter of time." He spread his palms in the gesture of the old bookseller in Czestochowa.

Heinz felt that his hands were shaking. He looked at the man with hatred, his fists clenched and ready to strike. Mecenas Agrest had seen men act that way before—screaming "Liar! It's not true!" and attacking friends and family. He put a hand on the young man's shoulder, lowering his voice to a murmur. "Wacek Konarski has gone over to the Partisans to fight beside those who risk their lives in acts of defiance and sabotage. Their courage is admirable, but it is futile, like all the rest. I could not tell you his whereabouts even if I knew."

Heinz had seen the corpses labeled "Partisan" hanging in public places, some of them mutilated. One day one of them would be carefree, laughing Wacek, his sparkling eyes glazed over with horror. Heinz bowed formally and said, "Thank you, Mecenas Agrest. I am sorry about your cousin."

He bit his lip and turned quickly away and made for the exit. There was no use waiting to hear more, and he wanted both to weep and to do something violent. He remembered his father's curses at the time his grandfather died. His new fear for Lilka and Wacek, pity for their grief and their danger opened wounds that had not healed, but had at least become familiar. He wanted revenge for his dead.

Wacek, the mischievous little brother who made faces at Adam when he talked seriously to Lilka, who was vain of his expensive toys and liked showing off and doing daring stunts to get attention; the handsome, silly youth, precociously bright but hopelessly undisciplined—Wacek was hiding somewhere in the city printing leaflets or setting fire to cars or smuggling guns and grenades, in constant danger of arrest and torture.

Heinz proceeded to the railway station, to get a suburban train, find the orphanage in Mydzieszyn, and find Lilka. He reached the little station at dusk. It was drab, nearly empty at that hour just before the curfew. Once it had been gay with weekenders and pleasure-seekers crowding out of the city toward the smart villas and hotels. There had been worried relatives laden with baskets for the patients of the sanatorium, pretty young socialite volunteers on their way to take the orphans for a day's outing. A well-dressed man, hurrying to get home before the curfew, glanced at Heinz and continued on his way. "Please, sir," Heinz called to him. "Do you know where I can get a room for tonight? I don't want to be caught here by the curfew."

The man looked him over cautiously. "Are you here to visit someone?"

Heinz saw no point in lying. "I'm trying to find an old girl friend, a Jewess. She is working at the Jewish orphange here. I am a Pole. I know it is foolhardy, but I am going to try."

The man smiled. "Foolhardy, yes. All right. Come with me. We can put you on a couch—and the back gate to the orphanage is just across the street from us. Guards have been known to take bribes in every country on earth." He winked knowingly. "Even those belonging to the superrace."

Heinz followed him, trying out various formulas of thanks. He poured out the story of his meeting with the young laborer in the café and with the lawyer, Agrest, omitting mention of Wacek. The man confirmed their stories. "The Jews are finished. The Nazi method is to starve them, then force them to betray each other. It is vile, but the love of life is powerful."

"Some are fighting back," said Heinz.

The man made a noncommittal sound. They arrived at a tall old building in the middle of the town and the man whistled a strange bird call. A window curtain moved on the second floor, and soon the door was opened by a thin, faded woman who looked as though she had once been pretty and stylish. Few words were exchanged, few explanations asked for. The woman set out soup and bread, and Heinz ate gratefully. He realized that he had not had any food all day. The woman refilled his plate, urging him to eat. Then she made up a bed on the couch, and wished him a good evening and Godspeed, since he was planning to leave at dawn, before his hosts were up. The man shook his hand solemnly. They had not asked his name, nor told him theirs. It was a strange kind of closeness, a brotherhood of phantoms.

Heinz could not sleep. He was thinking of Lilka, now only a few hundred yards away. It was still light, but everyone was ordered to remain indoors: the curfew had started at seven o'clock. Heinz decided to risk venturing outdoors wearing his Hitler Youth insignia. He hoped that he might catch a glimpse of Lilka, perhaps even exchange a greeting.

It was quiet on the streets. The dahlias in full bloom reminded him of the gardens in Polansk. He came to the gate, attended by a uniformed SS man smoking a cigarette. He looked at Heinz, noticed his swastika, and smiled. Heinz took his package of cigarettes and offered it to the guard, who accepted it without a word.

The building was only some five meters away from the gate. At the windows Heinz saw faces of the children and their nurses, thin, pale, and sickly. Then he noticed Lilka in her white frock and the white nurse's cap. At first she did not recognize him, but when he waved, she returned his greeting with a noncommittal smile, intended to conceal her surprise.

She disappeared and Heinz was afraid that he would not be able to see any more of her. Then she appeared at the door and approached the gate. They shook hands.

"Oh, Adam, I never expected to see you again. How . . . how . . ." Lilka had tears in her eyes. The guard, who did not want to be a close witness to the scene, turned his back.

"I came. I wanted . . . to see you."

She looked changed, slimmer and undernourished. Her black eyes contrasted even more strongly with her white skin. Her nurse's frock was mended in several places. On her left arm she wore an armband with a yellow Star of David. Heinz observed that all eyes in the windows were trained on them.

"May I walk with Fräulein! Just a few steps . . ." Heinz motioned to the windows and the many eyes watching them.

The guard nodded. "*Ja, ja macht schnell!*" (Make it fast!) he said in heavy accented German.

"What a surprise! I almost fainted. I could not believe my

eyes. Still, you know we all thought you had died. The execution, my God. . . . What happened?"

"I will tell you later."

They walked a few meters away. It began to get dark.

"I cannot get over it. I thought of you, Adam."

They walked in silence.

"Your mother?"

"She's dead, executed by the Nazis."

"My parents, too. You knew?"

Lilka nodded and took his hand.

"Are you afraid? Are you . . ."

"Not now. Not anymore, not for myself, for the children."

It was a warm July evening. No one was on the streets, no sounds of radios, now forbidden, disturbing the silence.

The sound of trucks interrupted the silence. The trucks halted in front of the gate. Armed, uniformed men were entering the gate.

"Oh God," Lilka cried. "I must return."

Both of them knew well what this meant.

Lilka tried to free her hand, but Heinz held on to it with all his strength. She struggled, crying, "I must. I must." She struggled to free herself but he was stronger. He twisted her arm behind her and led her away to the house where he was staying. On the stairs they halted in front of a window. The lights of the truck shown on the gate, the building, and the court in front of it. The line of children was already forming there, the oldest at the head and the youngest bringing up the rear. Some were fully dressed, others were still wearing their nightclothes with a sweater or a coat thrown over their shoulders. The guards counted them off and shoved them toward the vans. One boy broke the ranks and tried to run, and the nearest soldier knocked him down and kicked him viciously. The smaller children began to cry and hide their faces, but the guards thrust the line forward, shouting insults and slapping those that hung back. The attendants caressed the children and coaxed them to move forward quickly.

Lilka took hold of the window frame as though she would jump out, and shouted "Stop." She ran for the door, but Heinz seized her arm and twisted it behind her again. She struggled a moment, then sank to the floor, close to fainting. They heard the motors start up and the vans drive off. Lilka was sobbing in pain and fury and grief.

Later on no sounds came from where there was once the orphange. When Lilka stopped sobbing, Heinz, sitting next to her on the stairs, told her about the execution, his life in Nyphelheim. He did not reveal his plan to kill Hitler. Heinz was not sure whether Lilka understood him. From time to time she burst out in tears, moaning, "Children, my children . . . they will die, they will . . ."

With the first light of dawn they approached the window. The gate to the orphanage was open and the guard had gone. A man in the uniform of a Polish railroad employee was walking aimlessly about the courtyard, his head bowed in dejection.

Lilka recognized him. "It's Wacek . . . oh, Wacek. He must have heard about the . . . and he came to search for me."

XV

August 1942

There were tears and smiles when Lilka and Heinz met Wacek. The meeting did not last long. Wacek was afraid that they might be spotted by a Gestapo agent. He brought them without delay to the apartment of a fellow resistance fighter named Stach, another member of *Armia Krajowa*, the Home Army.

Stach was not home, but his toothless grandmother received them in the small kitchen. She fed them a breakfast of tea, pumpernickel, and eggs, but Lilka did not eat anything. Heinz had not seen Wacek since the beginning of the war. He remembered him as a child, a terrible tease who intruded on Heinz's courtship of Lilka. Now, Wacek, not quite seventeen, looked like a man, with long blond hair and a budding growth over his upper lip that might pass for a mustache.

The grandmother, who until that moment had hardly uttered a

word, asked them to behave as quietly as possible since the people living downstairs could not be trusted. She suggested that Lilka lie down on the sofa in the living room.

The two boys remained seated at the kitchen table. Wacek offered Heinz a Mewa cigarette. Lighting one himself, Wacek said, "It was after midnight when I heard about the liquidation at the orphanage. I was then at the Warsaw railroad station. I rushed immediately."

"Do you work for the railroad?" Heinz asked, wishing to change the subject.

"I have the papers of a railroad worker. *Pro forma.* I am a messenger for Armia Krajowa, carrying documents or orders from one unit to another."

Wacek extinguished his cigarette. "Lilka is still in danger. Could you get some Polish papers for her?" Heinz asked.

"That's easy. Sure. But it would not work. She still would want to . . . work in the ghetto. . . . I am afraid for her."

"But you can talk to her."

"It did not work before. She did have Polish papers, but you knew Mamusia, my mother, and Lilka . . ." Tears were in his eyes. He dried them with the sleeve of his navy-blue uniform. "Maybe you can persuade her. Otherwise the Gestapo, the bloody whores' sons, will kill her."

Heinz could understand Lilka. He also had witnessed the liquidation of the orphanage: the little boy kicked by the Gestapo beast, the small children pushed into the van. He did not hear Wacek now. He saw the vans, the children, and behind them a large portrait of Adolf Hitler, the one in the dining room in Nyphelheim: the Führer smiling. In Heinz's vision the portrait grew larger and larger—bigger than the vans, bigger than the orphanage building. *I will kill him. I will kill him with my own hand. I will . . .* Heinz vowed to himself. The drops of perspiration gathered on his forehead.

"What in hell is the matter with you? Are you getting sick?"

Heinz stood up and began to pace back and forth. Wacek, observing his excitement, snapped, "Sit down! We must be quiet. People downstairs . . . she warned us."

Shaking, Heinz sat down at the table. Wacek handed him a glass of water, which Heinz spilled while drinking.

The kitchen clock showed seven-fifteen. The curfew was over. One could hear the beginning of traffic on the street below. Some people were leaving the building.

"You must control your nerves. You got kind of soft hiding in those Kraut mountains."

Heinz remained tense and was ready to start pacing again but Wacek restrained him.

"What are we going to do about Lilka? I must save her," Heinz said.

"Perhaps she could live with a friend! Dr. Krzesniak?"

"I thought about it myself. But he is in danger, under Gestapo surveillance . . . . too dangerous for her and for him."

Lilka got up, but after her short nap she looked even worse than before. She still refused to eat and asked only for a glass of water. She answered all their questions with a short yes or no.

"We must do something—this is not the safest place to hide."

Lilka did not seem to be concerned, not even with the safety of her brother.

"I will try to get you some papers so you can at least move around." Then Wacek looked at Lilka searchingly. "Will you leave Warsaw? I could arrange for you to work in a hospital far away from here. Would you?"

"I don't know," she answered.

"Anyway, I will go out. I will try to get back here. If they do not stop me I will be back before the curfew."

After Wacek's departure Lilka went back to sleep on the sofa. Heinz settled down in a large plush chair where he tried to catch some sleep.

But he could not sleep. He began to imagine that the real Adolf Hitler was watching the liquidation of the orphanage. He is standing there smiling, with the expression of a man pleased with his accomplishments. Heinz then came forward in his Hitler Youth uniform to salute the Führer. Instead he pulled a knife and stabbed him.

Lilka and Heinz waited for Wacek until curfew time. He did not come. Toward evening Lilka ate some bread and then went to sleep again. Heinz returned to his thoughts about Hitler, now somewhere on the Russian Front, at a safe distance from the fighting line. Heinz arrived with a group of his schoolmates from Nyphelheim, each armed with a rifle. Heinz suddenly faced the Führer, raised his rifle, and shot him between the eyes.

In the morning there was still no news from Wacek. At four o'clock that afternoon Stach appeared. He was a big man in his late twenties.

"I have a message for you two from Wacek." He pulled an envelope from his pocket. Heinz opened it hurriedly. It contained a document for a German girl, aged sixteen, in the name of Maria Werner. The photo, however, bore no resemblance to Lilka. There was a short note attached:

"This is the best I could do at the moment. I am still trying."

Stach, like his grandmother, did not say much, a characteristic that must have made him a valuable member in the organization. Soon after the meal of pea soup and some potato pancakes, Stach and his grandmother retired.

Heinz sat with Lilka at the same kitchen table where he had talked with her brother the day before. "Will you take a job in Zakopane?" Heinz asked.

"I still don't know. I am not quite sure I will be able to function here. All these horrors."

Heinz clasped his hands to his head. "You are in shock, but you must understand. You must save yourself," he said loudly, frustrated by Lilka's refusal to understand.

"How can you . . ." Heinz persisted.

Lilka put her finger in front of her mouth. "Please!" she said. "The people downstairs will hear you." She looked sadly at Heinz, breathed deeply, and said, "I still remember you as the boy with the best manners. I loved to dance with you."

"That was ages ago. Now we must forget it."

"Oh, no, on the contrary, we must remember. This was the nicest part of our lives. Remember! You gave me a gold bracelet. I wore it until just recently."

"Yes, I remember. And you kissed me then."

They talked well beyond midnight, recalling those precious events of the years before the war.

There was still no sign of Wacek. At five in the afternoon Stach returned with a man called Jozek.

"We must clear out right away." Stach's message was meant for all of them, including his grandmother. "They caught Franek, another member of the Underground. They will torture him. We are not sure how much he will tell."

Stach and his companion began removing some electronic equipment that had been hidden under the sofa and packing it into their rucksacks. "You can still catch the five forty-seven train to Warsaw. It would be safer for you," Stach told Heinz and Lilka. "I will take care of grandmother."

"But Wacek?" Heinz asked.

"I don't know where he lives. He will get in touch with you. Don't try to come here again. The Gestapo will catch you."

In a few moments Heinz and Lilka were ready. Heinz knew the way to the railroad station. They passed by the gate, still open. Within there was no sign of life. In front of the yard, lying in the dirt, was an armband with a small yellow Star of David. Shaken, Lilka fumbled for Heinz's hand.

The train halted at every station, and at each stop new crowds pushed their way into the cars. Heinz managed to hold on to his position near the window. He was standing near Lilka. The mob pushed him so close to Lilka that he could feel her heartbeat against his breast. With his body he tried to shield her against the pressure of the crowds. Lilka and Heinz looked at each other, their eyes only inches apart.

"I feel safe here with you," she whispered. Her frail body was leaning against his.

"The people are pushing . . . there are no more places," Heinz said. "They, too, must travel . . . They may have as good reasons as ours."

He looked at her eyes, lighted by the afternoon sun entering the car through the opened windows. They were dark blue, like the cornflowers they used to pick during the last summer before the war. Once, when they had gathered a large bunch, she had woven a crown of these flowers for him.

The train was passing the same fields where the cornflowers had grown wild. How he would like to leave this train and walk there with Lilka! The aroma of hay permeated the air.

"You smiled. Why?" Lilka asked.

"I forgot the present . . . just for a moment," Heinz took her hand. "I wanted to invite you to pick the cornflowers."

"As you can see, the grass was cut. . . . I would have loved to join you."

After their arrival in Warsaw they walked, with thousands of other passengers, into the station. Nobody paid any attention to them.

"What can we do now?" Heinz asked.

"You must return to your school."

"But what will happen to you?"

The station was packed with hundreds of people: those who knew they would not be able to get home before the curfew, and others whose trains were to depart after that deadline. The people in the crowd seemed accustomed to being here. They argued, talked, and even shouted upon seeing a friend or an acquaintance. Some groups formed to organize a party and share a bottle of vodka or *bimber*, the so-called homemade alcohol. The ventilation was very poor. It was hot and it smelled of cheap tobacco and human sweat.

Heinz and Lilka found an empty spot near a wall where they sat down on the bare floor. Heinz looked at her face and noticed how different she appeared from all the other women in the crowd. Lilka did not smile but expressed the pain which the events of the last several hours had engraved on her face. Was she now thinking about her future or reliving the sight of the children entering the van? Heinz could not tell. She was silent, her eyes focused on the floor.

Heinz took Lilka's hand; it felt cold and lifeless. He wanted to tell her how sorry he was but decided against it. He noticed a commotion that started at the far end of the station. The German police had entered the building. The people stopped talking; the noise turned into silence. Ten policemen in steel helmets divided into units and began asking everyone to show his identification papers. Heinz could hear their voices: "*Ausweis!*" (Passport!)

Lilka heard these voices. Two policemen were only a few meters away; they were approaching Heinz and Lilka.

"They look like . . . they are the same who took my child," she whispered, her body shaking. Her face turned a bluish-gray; drops of perspiration appeared on her forehead. Her body began to shake. She was close to fainting.

Heinz helped her to get up. They were facing the policemen.

Heinz presented his *Kennkarte*, with a swastika, marked Volksdeutsche. The policeman did not open it and returned it to Heinz.

"What are you doing here?" he asked. "There is a waiting room reserved for the Germans."

One of the policemen, a tall muscular man in his twenties, took Lilka by the arm and helped her toward the waiting room. On the doors was the sign "*Nur für Deutsche*" (Only for Germans). The room, spacious with plush seats, had served before the war as the first-class waiting room. Only one elderly couple was there now, sitting at a table drinking beer. The policeman helped Lilka to a chair, called the waiter, and requested a glass of water for her.

"You should call a doctor," he said. "She needs medical attention."

"She is just tired," Heinz said. "She will be all right, it is the heat."

After the policeman left and Lilka finished her glass of water, they remained silent for a while. A group of uniformed soldiers entered and ordered beer. None of them was much older than Heinz. They glanced from time to time at Lilka and exchanged some remarks in whispers. Suddenly, a scream was heard: "*Bitte, bitte.*" (Please, please.) The soldiers laughed. Lilka looked at Heinz. They both understood what was going on: someone was pleading for his life. The wrong kind of papers might mean death. Lilka's body shook. She had tears in her eyes.

Heinz took her hand. It felt warm and moist.

"Tomorrow morning we will leave," Heinz said.

Lilka nodded.

"We will go to see Father Sebastian. He will help us."

"It does not matter to me."

"Father Sebastian has connections," Heinz continued. "He could find a place for you to live."

Heinz, once having conceived the idea to seek Father Sebastian's help, was becoming enthusiastic with the prospect of seeing him again. Heinz still remembered Father Sebastian's advice about not coming to Poland, but he knew he would be forgiven.

Lilka closed her eyes. After a while she started to breathe regularly. Heinz got a blanket from a waiter and covered her. Heinz also got some sleep sitting next to Lilka.

Lilka and Heinz took the train at ten-thirty in the morning for Czestochowa and arrived there in the early afternoon. They walked through the poplar-lined Aleja, passed near the monastery, and turned into St. Barbara Street, full of stalls where blue and white statues of the Madonna, religious prints, and prayer books were for sale.

Number 33, where Father Sebastian lived, was an old two-storied house. The stairs were dark and narrow, with a damp, fusty smell.

After Heinz had knocked at the door for a while, it was opened by a thin man in his seventies with a bald head and dressed in a flannel robe.

"What do you want?" the man asked, exposing his toothless mouth. His gray face was covered with short whiskers.

"We came to visit Father . . ." Heinz said. "Father Sebastian."

"I will see," the man said and shut the door in front of them.

Heinz and Lilka exchanged glances. Heinz felt uneasy.

He heard a series of quick steps behind the door. The door opened. Father Sebastian at first did not recognize them in the darkness of the stairs.

"What may I do . . . Oh God, there, that's you . . . and this is Lilka, Lilka Konarski." He embraced both of them.

"Oh, what a blessing that you have come. . . . Thank God, that you are here. Come in!"

The corridor was narrow and it smelled of cooked cabbage.

Father Sebastian led the way to his room. It was furnished with a bed, two chairs, and on the white walls hung an iron crucifix.

Father Sebastian appeared to Heinz to be somewhat smaller than he remembered him. His hair was grayer and his face thinner. His gray eyes remained lively.

Father Sebastian sat down on the edge of the bed, inviting Heinz and Lilka to sit in the chairs.

"God must have answered my prayers. . . . I worried about you, my boy . . . about both of you."

"I had to come here . . ." Heinz began to mumble.

"He was homesick," Lilka said. "You will forgive him, Father?"

"It's all right, my boy," Father Sebastian said. "I made a suggestion, but times change. I am overjoyed to see both of you."

"Lilka is in danger, Father. She must hide. We need . . ."

"With every day it is more difficult to stay alive," Father Sebastian said. He turned to Lilka. "There is a rumor going around that the ghetto here might be liquidated soon. But I will find a safe place for both of you, so please don't worry now."

"But, Father, I will go back to school." It is only from the Oberschule that I can carry out my plan, Heinz thought.

"We will discuss the plans later. Now you will share with me my meal. . . . You may stay here tonight, or if it is necessary, longer."

They ate in a small dining room with a wooden table and chairs. In the background stood a red plush sofa. The main course was a cabbage soup with plenty of dark bread. The meal was served by the same old man who had opened the door for them. During dinner Father Sebastian discussed his only hobby: collecting postcards. His collection had already reached five thousand and he promised to show it some other time.

After dinner Lilka went to sleep in Father Sebastian's room, while Heinz remained in the dining room with Father Sebastian.

"Lilka is close to a breakdown," Father Sebastian said.

"Can you find a place in the country, Father?"

"Country, village, fields are not safe for hiding. A new person becomes conspicuous, easily noticed. Questions are raised, suspicions voiced. There is always a danger that the newcomer will be betrayed by a jealous neighbor, thinking that the host is getting rich. You know the penalty for hiding the Jews—death."

The narrow window of the room remained open. Heinz could hear the voices of children playing and the distant barking of a dog.

"No, I have a different plan," Father Sebastian said. "For both of you."

"But, Father, I must return to my school."

"The school may no longer be a safe place for you."

"Why, Father, why?"

"The Germans are still searching for the papers once hidden by your father."

"They will never be able to find them. The papers are hidden in the beet field. Ten meters north of the linden tree. I had to tell you . . ."

"What concerns me now is that they could discover your true identity."

"How could they?"

"They are trying. They had a young man, named Andreas Wendel . . ."

"But he is my best friend!"

"Exactly! That is why they, whoever they are, used him."

"But Andreas . . ."

"He may have been blackmailed into working for them. Anyway, he was in Katowice checking the Heinz Hauptmann dossiers."

Heinz was so stunned by this information that he poured himself a glass of water and drank it in one gulp. Father Sebastian stood up, walked to the window and shut it.

Father Sebastian continued, after returning to his seat, "Hauptmann is a common name. The real Heinz Hauptmann could have used a false birth certificate . . . that's what the Germans found on his body. Still, this may furnish them with a needed lead. . . . No, I don't think it would be safe to go back."

"Father, I really must." Heinz thought that whatever plan Father Sebastian made for him would make the accomplishing of his mission impossible.

"My boy, this is why I was so happy to see you. Frankly, I was ready to get in touch with you to warn you. It is so lucky that you are here. . . . Now listen to me! In Lwow there is an institute headed by Professor Wajgel, who discovered during the previous war an injection immunizing a person against typhoid fever. It is a dreadful disease spread by lice. Many German soldiers are dying of it. The Poles who work there have a measure of protection not accorded to others."

"But, Father, I don't know any biology."

"You don't need to. Besides, a friend of mine could employ and train both of you. He has done me that favor before. I can trust him."

Heinz began to think about his living in Lwow, seeing Lilka every day, being with Poles and living without the Oberschule discipline. But living there he would no longer be able to travel in the Third Reich. He would be far away from all sources of information. He would never be able to kill the man responsible for the death of his parents.

"Father, I think that's wonderful for Lilka, but I . . . I will have to return to my school."

"But, why, my boy, why? The original purpose of studying there was to hide from the Germans' persecution. No, you will be safer here."

"I must go there. I will graduate in just a few months."

"You may be drafted."

"There is still some unfinished business for me, Father."

"You could do so much here, Heinz. You can join the Home Army . . . like I did."

"The Underground will not be able to change the course of the war." Heinz stood up. He began to pace the small room. "Hitler will continue his executions. . . . He will wipe us out before this war is won by the Allies, and if . . ."

"You must have faith that we will win. In the Far East, Japan attacked, and for the first time the Allies stopped the aggression and are defending their positions. Americans landed on Guadalcanal. One day they will land in Western Europe."

"By that time half or more of us will have been slaughtered by Hitler."

"This is why we need young people like you to join the Home Army. We must show the Germans that we are strong. That's the only way for us to get their respect. When they learn our strength, they might stop the mass murder."

Heinz did not comment. Heinz loved Poland, but he did not believe that by joining the Underground he could contribute to Polish victory. He knew the way to achieve that goal—killing Hitler.

"There are many tasks for the Home Army for which you could be essential. You excellent knowledge of German could be exploited. We need you here."

Heinz did not listen. He sat down at the table. "I must go back to school," he said.

Father Sebastian stood up and began pacing the floor. "The Germans are now occupying a large part of Russia, but they are far from victory. The soldiers returning from the front for their furloughs are disenchanted. They are no longer the same young men, full of enthusiasm. You know the war may end unexpectedly. There are persistent rumors of plots to overthrow Hitler. Some men from Hitler's inner circle might be involved."

Heinz, hearing about the potential plot on Hitler, began to shake.

"It is getting late. We will talk tomorrow. You can sleep on the couch and I will go to the monastery before the curfew."

"But I will go back to school, Father."

"We will discuss it tomorrow. You must remember that Lilka needs you. In her condition it would be hard for her to survive alone. She needs someone she can trust. Someone like you."

Father Sebastian went into the living room and sat by a small fire. He fell slowly to sleep, tortured by visions of death and a conquered Poland.

Meanwhile, Heinz crept quietly to the door of Lilka's room. He opened the door, walked over to the bed where she slept, and tenderly shook her awake. "You must get up," he said. "We are taking the train to Nyphelheim."

Heinz slowly picked up his luggage and was ready to open the door when the last words he had heard from Father Sebastian echoed in his mind: "She needs someone she can trust. Someone like you." She would join him in his trip to Nyphelheim. She could stay with Kotecha. After all, Kotecha had saved Heinz's life once.

XVI

September, October 1942

They took the train at 11:30 P.M. Their papers were checked only once on the train. The border policeman looked at Lilka, glanced at her papers, uttered "*In Ordnung*" (In order) and left their compartment. Heinz bought food: wiener sausages, bread and lemonade, but Lilka refused to eat. In Vienna they had to change for a train going to Salzburg. There was a wait of more than three hours. They sat in the waiting room, where Lilka finally ate some bread and drank some coffee. From the station in Nyphelheim they had to walk the four kilometers to the Oberschule. Heinz could travel this distance in less than half an hour, but with Lilka in her weakened condition, it took them more than an hour.

They reached Kotecha's basement apartment just before midnight. A narrow beam of light, visible through curtains, indicated that Kotecha was at home and still up. Heinz knocked at the door.

Kotecha was pleased to see Heinz and shook his hand with all his force. When he saw Lilka, he asked Heinz, "You have brought me a patient?"

Heinz nodded.

Kotecha put the kettle on the electric stove. Without a word he started to make a bed up for Lilka.

"My wife is now helping my daughter in Prague," Kotecha said. "My daughter has two small baby boys. Her husband is away in . . ." Kotecha turned to Heinz. "I will be able to take care of your young friend, at least for a while."

Then he mixed a glass of hot linden tea with several spoons of honey and handed it to Lilka.

"Drink it, please! It will help you."

Lilka obeyed and sipped the brew with a spoon. Kotecha pulled from under his bed a valise, opened it, and took out a poppy-seed cake. He gave each of them a large piece.

"I used to love it . . . I love it now," Lilka said. "I like being here."

"It makes me so happy," Heinz said. "You know, Lilka lived through so . . ."

"You don't have to tell me, Heinz," Kotecha interrupted him. "I know it. Let's finish the cake and then to bed. Sleep is the best doctor."

After Heinz said good night to Lilka, Kotecha accompanied him on his walk to the dormitory. It was a clear summer night with all the stars shining.

"Your friend Lilka is in a state of shock. She will need rest and care. I think she can get them here. But for a long time she still will be vulnerable. Any sudden bad news or new experience may cause a relapse. Let's hope it won't occur."

"Why should anything like that happen here? Here in Nyphelheim?"

"Well, I don't know. I worry now . . . about you." Kotecha stopped and scratched his forehead. "Lilka will be all right. Nobody drops by into my basement. Anyway, I could always explain. . . . They will think she is my duaghter. But you . . . you, Heinz . . ."

"Oh, I will be all right."

"I am still worrying. Things are happening here." Kotecha put his arm on Heinz's shoulder. "Stranger things. I see Dr. Neufeind frightened. I saw him a few times talking to your fat friend, Piersohn. Always hiding." Kotecha remained silent for a moment. "You know, Heinz, you should stay away from Lilka for a while, for her sake. If she needs you I will tell you. I will get in touch."

They talked for almost an hour. Finally Heinz thanked Kotecha, bid him good night, and made his way back to the dormitory.

Two days later Andreas returned to school. He greeted Heinz warmly, but Heinz immediately saw the change that had come over his companion since he had seen him last. Andreas had lost weight; his face was drawn, and despite the weeks of vacation he looked as if he had not slept a night through for a long time. In place of his usual exuberance and enthusiasm were a sadness and dejection that even someone less familiar with Andreas would have recognized immediately. Above all, he turned aside any questions about his summer and what had happened to him since he had last seen his friend.

When he spoke it was as though he were reciting word for word the contents of the Nazi newspapers. And he found an opportunity to refer to an uncle in the Gestapo he had never mentioned in all their acquaintance. He expected to see this uncle soon, Andreas said, for he would be traveling in the Führer's entourage to Berchtesgaden. It was on trips like this, Andreas explained, that the Gestapo was under the most pressure since security for the Führer was most difficult to maintain while traveling. He pointed out the danger of some suicidal maniac jumping on the moving train with a bomb, grenade, or some weapon to destroy the Führer.

Andreas told Heinz he had traveled on the Führer's private train this summer with his uncle. He described the fortified cars in great detail, volunteering the information that the first car after the locomotive was the car with the antiaircraft guns, that the individual cars themselves were armored, while the Führer's personal car was equipped with steel shutters that could be lowered to cover all the windows in seconds. As for the Führer's private quarters, said Andreas, they were something to admire, with luxurious meeting rooms, a plush salon, a sleeping compartment, and a washroom with full-size tub. As if to authenticate his report, he mentioned the number of his personal car—10215.

Heinz could not help but notice that Andreas was as interested in Heinz's reactions to all the wonders he described as he was in the wonders themselves. He was nervous and awkward, and as he spoke his eyes gazed all about, carefully avoiding contact with his friend's eyes.

Andreas declared himself an aficionado of the train. Repeatedly he referred to his apprehension that someone could jump on the train in the darkness, enter the window of the Führer's car, and possibly murder the great leader. "A single deranged individual could do it," Andreas declared, "even though the Führer's movements are top secret and the route of his train is never determined until the last minute to minimize the danger from assassins." Further, how would an assassin know the exact location of the Führer's car, seventh or eighth in a twelve- to fourteen-car train!

It was clear to Heinz that all of this was being done for his benefit. Andreas' interest in the train was too convenient to be a coincidence. His awkward presentation of the facts was unbelievable. But why was he giving Heinz this information? He certainly knew about the missing crossbow. Surely the Gestapo's investigation must have led to the Wendels. Was it possible he shared Heinz's desire to see Hitler dead? Through this jumble of intrigue and suspicion, Heinz felt his friend's fear. In Andreas' once lively eyes, he saw a specter of violence looming over the boy, bearing down on him, haunting his every step. Like an animal cornered by a hunter, Andreas was frantic, terrified by the appearance of a power far greater than his own.

Heinz longed to reach out to his friend, to transport both of them back in time to the forest where they had walked together. He decided he would confront Andreas, and tell him his plan to kill Hitler. He had nothing to lose. Since Andreas already knew, the Gestapo must know too. It would help Heinz to know exactly how much they knew. But why hadn't they arrested him? Perhaps Andreas could solve the puzzle. Heinz did not know whether his concern was for his plan or for his friend whose burden he longed to share.

One evening, about a week after Andreas' arrival at school, the boys were walking through the yard. They were chatting casually about a new teacher when suddenly Heinz looked directly at Andreas and said, "What is it, Andreas? Why are you frightened?"

Andreas was taken aback and tried to remain casual, but even this gentle attack on his charade had penetrated his defenses. His voice quavered as he answered, "Frightened? What are you talking about, Heinz?" He looked quickly away.

"I'm talking about your new-found uncle in the Gestapo. Your fascination with Hitler's train," said Heinz, putting his hands on Andreas' shoulders and turning him to face him. In this gesture there was both urgency and compassion. Assassin and friend were reaching out.

Andreas was scared. His face went white, and he trembled slightly. "The Gestapo knows your true identity," he said, looking first at the ground and then into Heinz's eyes." Heinz was confused. With his hands still on Andreas' shoulders, he shook him firmly and said, "But why haven't they arrested me, Andreas?" The two boys had walked from the schoolyard into the woods surrounding the Oberschule. The night was coming on and an owl hooted in the distance.

"They think you're working for some Party members who want Hitler dead. But they don't know you're an assassin. They think you're just a functionary," Andreas said, beginning to sob softly. "They hope you'll lead them to the other people involved. Piersohn's working with a group that wants Himmler in power. He discovered your mission, and decided to have you kill Hitler for them. That way there would be no way of connecting Piersohn with Hitler's death."

"But how did the Gestapo find out about my identity?" Heinz said.

"Piersohn told them," Andreas answered. "They offered a reward for information about the papers. But Piersohn's a fool. He'll never get any money from the Gestapo. It was Piersohn who suggested that they not arrest you right away, that you might lead them to the Himmler people. But the Gestapo doesn't take many chances, Heinz, especially not with Hitler's life. They'll arrest you before too long."

"But if Piersohn wants Hitler assassinated, why would he take the chance of the Gestapo arresting me before I could kill him? It doesn't make sense."

"It does if you know Piersohn," Andreas said. "He's a very careful man. And his only commitment is to himself. He doesn't really care whether you kill Hitler or not, he's just protecting himself on all sides. He needs friends in the Gestapo and in the Himmler faction."

"But why, Andreas?" asked Heinz. "You must have helped them put the crossbow puzzle together."

"Yes I did, Heinz. I told them about the woman who stopped you on the street and recognized you as Adam Leski. I was scared, Heinz. Please forgive me. Piersohn made me give you the information about the train."

Heinz was beside himself with grief. He felt a profound sense of betrayal.

"Heinz," said Andreas, looking sadly at him. "He threatened to have my brother killed if I didn't co-operate."

Heinz looked at Andreas with compassion. His anger was gone. Driven to the edge of despair, Andreas had betrayed his friend to save his brother. Heinz saw him now as still another victim of the Nazis. An old proverb about our misfortunes being blessings in disguise came into his mind. Heinz thought it strange at first, but quickly grasped its meaning. He now knew all there was to know of Hitler's train.

There was no time to waste. He set off quickly through the woods, leaving a devastated Andreas behind.

That night, as Heinz was preparing to flee the school, he was displeased to see the roundish figure of Kotecha emerge at the end of the long corridor near the dining room.

Kotecha passed Heinz, whispering in his ear, "Come to see me this evening."

Heinz had known that Kotecha would take good care of Lilka. With all his attention focused on his mission, he had forgotten about her. Now, hearing Kotecha's message, he feared that some complication had arisen that might interfere with his plans.

When Heinz arrived that evening in Kotecha's basement room, Lilka and her host were sitting at the table drinking tea. Tarot cards were arranged on the table and Heinz knew that Kotecha had been telling fortunes, perhaps Lilka's. The pallor of Lilka's face had changed to a healthy reddish-tan one gets from the mountain air, sun, and wind. She had gained weight. Also, she wore a dress that Heinz had not seen before: navy-blue chiffon with a white collar.

"Pan Kotecha is predicting a journey for me," Lilka said. "I have had devils in my past, and there is a knight in my future."

"Her dreams and wishes will be fulfilled," Kotecha said, winking with his left eye at Heinz behind Lilka's back.

"Good dreams, I hope," Heinz said.

"Oh, don't worry. I dream now of flowers, cornflowers or edelweiss," Lilka said. Then she focused her eyes on Heinz. "I see myself, in my dream, among people, free people, singing on their streets, laughing happy people."

"Well, Heinz, I asked you here to talk to you," Kotecha said, serving Heinz a glass of tea. "How can we help her to make these dreams come true?"

"Oh, yes, Heinz. Pan Kotecha is the greatest dreamer. . . . He told me that I could perhaps one day . . . in Switzerland the people live the same lives as before the war—free of fear."

"But Switzerland . . . the border is well guarded," Heinz said. "It is impossible."

"Nothing is impossible," Kotecha contradicted him.

Heinz felt annoyed with Kotecha for making such unrealistic promises to Lilka. The Swiss border had been watched since the beginning of the war with units of the Gestapo deployed along its entire length. "The risk would be high," he said.

"Heinz is a realist," Lilka interjected. Then, turning her face to

Heinz, she said, "Don't spoil our dreams. Possible or impossible, it does not matter. The idea is so beautiful when I think of it."

Heinz decided not to argue the point any longer. He joined in the tea-drinking ceremony. Kotecha told him how he was taking Lilka on long walks through the fields and mountains, looking for mushrooms and collecting autumn flowers.

That night Kotecha walked with Heinz on the way back to the dormitory. "You see, Heinz," Kotecha said, trying to catch up with Heinz, "she must get away from here. She has recovered some, but it is temporary. Anything, any bad news, can finish her. She told me everything about her life. I want to help her."

"Switzerland is impossible. You know it yourself."

"But impossible things happen. You survived."

"That's different. No, Switzerland, it . . ."

"Then you would want to see her die in a concentration camp?"

"No, but she may live here."

"How long do you think it will be possible! People will start asking questions."

They were approaching the dormitory. Kotecha put his arm on Heinz's shoulder. He wanted to continue this conversation.

"She could return to Poland, to rejoin her brother," Heinz said. He began to grow angry at Kotecha's interference. All this talk of Kotecha's concern for Lilka only disturbed his own dreams.

"To see more tragedy, atrocities, death?" Kotecha took his arm from Heinz's shoulder. "You know that she would have another nervous breakdown, maybe the first day there."

Heinz did not worry about his own future. He accepted the risk of his own death as the price of killing the Führer. But he could not help Lilka now. The Gestapo was onto him; he had to kill Hitler quickly.

"Well, I cannot help her, not with Switzerland," he said.

"Maybe you could. I am going to investigate." Kotecha took Heinz's hand. "For you, Heinz, especially for you—escape there is a must."

"Not for me. But if you could help her I would be grateful."

"But you also must help."

"I will try," Heinz said without conviction.

When Heinz reached his room around midnight, Andreas was asleep. When he was in bed, he could not help thinking about his trip with Lilka on the train to Warsaw. How he had tried to protect her from the crowds and how his helping her had made him happy. He remembered looking into Lilka's eyes, feeling her warmth and closeness.

That night Heinz dreamed of trains and Lilka, of tree-lined boulevards crowded with people, some of them singing. Heinz and Lilka were singing too.

Then other images appeared. . . . He was on a white horse, riding parallel to a moving train. A window opened. He drew the saber from its scabbard at his side. He was some place in the mountains, and cold rain drizzled down and yellow leaves were falling from chestnut trees. Then these images faded and others appeared. He was younger, an eager boy. Somehow he knew the year: 1938. But he rode on the same white horse, up to a large white house where a great celebration was under way. His father met him on the threshold and welcomed him with open arms, telling him, "We are rejoicing over the news of the passing of the monster. Where were you?" When Adam hesitated, unable to tell him, his father continued, "But that is unimportant. Please come and join us."

In the massive dining room a large table was covered with white cloths and loaded with bowls full of steaming meats, vegetable dishes, and pastries. Many people sat at the feast, laughing, joking, and singing.

Adam recognized Dr. Konarski sitting at one end of the table. As soon as the doctor saw Adam arriving he got up and shook his hand. And Pani Magda was playing Adam's favorite Chopin waltz at the piano. Adam saw Lilka at the other end of the table. Before he could go to her, his mother appeared and embraced him. She was weeping with joy. "There will be no more wars," his mother said. "We are all so happy. You must enjoy this great feast. You must be hungry. You haven't eaten for a long time. Here is a plate of the best *bigos* I ever made."

His father came up to him, holding a big glass of *Starka.*

"This is the one I was saving for a special, unique occasion," he said. "Go ahead and drink it. I waited twenty-five years for it to age. You must toast our guests."

The music of the waltz continued to play, and Heinz saw Lilka dancing gracefully with a young lieutenant. She took every opportunity to turn her head to meet Adam's eyes. He could tell she wanted to say something to him.

Then someone shook him. Heinz woke up. It was Andreas. "Time to get up," Andreas said. He was dressed for the morning calisthenics: black shorts, white cotton T-shirt.

It was a clear morning. Heinz would have preferred to return to bed and dream more about Polansk, his parents, Lilka. Reluctantly he began to focus on reality.

"I have some news," Andreas said. "You would be interested to hear . . . the Führer will come to Munich in November—next month."

"Thank you, Andreas. You have helped me," Heinz said gratefully to his friend.

The whistle sounded and the boys ran out of the room, hurriedly putting the bed linen on the sill of the open window. Running along the corridor Andreas whispered, "He will be traveling by train."

As he was on his way down the steps to morning exercises, Heinz was stopped by a fellow student who told him that a woman was waiting in front of their dormitory and that she wanted to see him. Heinz knew that this must be an emergency. He ran down the stairs to meet Else.

As soon as they walked far enough not to be heard by anyone, Else said, "Last night Willi arrived here in Nyphelheim."

It hurt Heinz now to hear the name of Else's husband and to learn that he was here.

"He's going to arrest you, Heinz," Else continued. Else still had difficulty catching her breath. "You must leave at once."

"We can't talk here," Heinz said. "You go now. I'll meet you at the dry-cleaning place in an hour. Remember, you still have the key. You be waiting there for me."

Heinz ran to his room. Hurriedly, he packed all his belongings. Pulling the image of the Black Madonna from under the mattress and putting it in his wallet, he rushed through the corridors and down the stairs. At the bottom Heinz encountered Neufeind.

"Where are you rushing? I want to talk to you. I have to. It is important," the professor said.

"I am sorry."

Heinz ran past him and out of the building. He heard Neufeind's irregular steps behind him, but the limping teacher could not catch up with an athletic schoolboy. Neufeind called after him, "Stop, please stop." The distance between them was lengthening and shortly Neufeind's appeals were no longer audible to Heinz.

Else was waiting at the door of the dry-cleaning store.

"Heinz, you must rush. We cannot talk," she said.

"I am ready to leave."

Heinz was standing close to Else. He took her in his arms. He smelled the violets. "But not quite ready to leave you now," he said.

Else had a camel's-hair coat on. Quivering, he helped her to take it off and spread it on the floor. His fingers shook. Heinz could not open the buttons on her blouse. Else helped him. When he had entered her and moved his body with hers, he repeated, "I love you. I love you."

Everything melted away and he was in Poland, on his way back to Polansk with Else. He pictured himself walking with her up the front steps of the big old house and proudly drawing her through the doorway with him, wondering what his mother would say.

When his mother and father rushed forward to meet them, he introduced her. "This is my fiancée, Fräulein von Enzian." The little "von" in front of her name should be a good recommendation. After all, one of the grandmothers, Adam could not remember which, had a name with the little "von."

"Heinz, you will have to get up," Else said when it was over. She kissed him. "I am sorry, *Liebling*, but you must leave."

Slowly he became aware of the need to escape. He stood up.

"Walk through the woods as much as you can," she said. "Then try to catch a train to Munich from some small station."

Else came to embrace him. "I will miss you," she said.

"So will I miss you."

After he had left her and was walking through the narrow streets of Nyphelheim, the aroma of violets stayed with him.

Following Else's instructions, he kept to the woods. He walked the whole night, ate some food from his rucksack, then continued his march during the day.

He knew that he should avoid the larger stations in the area. They would be logical places for the police to search. Still he knew he would have to pass through one of the big transit stations. He was familiar with the terminal at Munich. In order to avoid entering the station, Heinz decided to jump from the train before reaching there.

He started out walking in search of a road where he could look for a car or truck to take him to any station where he could continue his escape by rail.

As Heinz emerged from the woods it was already dark, but he was able to follow a narrow winding road that, after about an hour, brought him to a small town. He encountered little traffic on this road, nothing more than a small Volkswagen and a half-truck. As he entered the narrow streets he stopped in front of a small inn, where he saw the half-truck that had passed him and the driver already returning to his vehicle.

"Where are you going?" he asked the driver. "I need a ride."

"I am heading for Munich," the driver told him. The truck was loaded with crates on the seat next to him. He told Heinz that the regular truck was being repaired and he had to overload this small vehicle. The driver added, however, that there might be some space in the back under the rubberized tarpaulin. It would be very uncomfortable there, he told Heinz, but a young man could manage.

After they had ridden for little more than a few blocks, Heinz, from where he lay squeezed between the crates with a strong smell of fresh fish, heard the loud command, "Halt!" Then he heard a voice asking the driver to identify his cargo.

"Just fish," the driver said, "just fish; some small, some big, mountain *Forelle* (trout)."

The same voice asked the driver whether he had seen a young man of Heinz's physical description.

No, the driver told him, he had not.

The voice continued, warning the driver that a very dangerous criminal was roaming the area. Should such a stranger ask for a lift, it should be reported immediately. The driver would be well rewarded for performing such a patriotic duty, he was told. After that conversation, the truck drove off, at first slowly, then gaining speed. The driver must have chosen the worst road in Germany. Heinz had trouble holding on to the crates, wet from the rain. The smell of fish nauseated him. After a few hours that seemed endless, the truck started a steep descent. The rain beat hard on the tarpaulin, giving Heinz the feeling that he was in a boat, slowly sinking to the bottom of the ocean.

Heinz recalled the friendly face of the driver and was surprised that the owner of this face was capable of such a wild drive. As he clung to the crates, the truck suddenly came to a rough stop and Heinz heard the voice of the driver shouting to him, "*'raus!*" Heinz climbed down from his perch and saw that the driver had picked a road lined only by farmland to get rid of him.

"Just get out of here!" the driver told him. "I don't want to see the likes of you again."

"I am grateful for what you have done for me."

"I don't want your gratitude. You almost got me into big trouble with the damn Gestapo," the driver snapped. "Just disappear and leave me alone!"

Then he drove away.

Heinz started walking in the direction the truck had taken. In spite of all he had been through it was pleasant to be walking alone in the countryside glistening from the recent rain.

In little more than fifteen minutes he saw a sign that told him he was only five kilometers from Prien. Pacing himself, he reached the main road and civilization, but not before his head started aching from fatigue and hunger. He had spent the last twenty-four hours outdoors; and he was cold to the bone.

Approaching Prien he sighted a sign for a Café Obermaier and he hurried toward it. Entering a large room, he was greeted by the warmth from an open fireplace where a single big log glowed on the hearth. At scattered tables there were a few couples, uniformed men with their women. At a large table in a corner a few men were drinking beer. A radio was playing classical music.

A headwaiter in his sixties sat at the entrance reading *Völkischer Beobachter*. He looked at Heinz as if he were expecting him. He immediately resumed his reading.

Heinz chose the empty table nearest the fire and accepted a menu from a young blond waitress. He noted that the menu stipulated beside the price of each item the required number of ration coupons. Fortunately he had meat and bread coupons so he chose pea soup with pigs' ears: there was no requirement of the meat ration for this soup. The pigs' ears did not apparently qualify as meat. Then he ordered the pork schnitzel with Bavarian *Kartoffelknödel*, a kind of potato dumpling. Heinz split his bread coupons, ordering one slice of white bread and two slices of pumpernickel.

The music stopped and Heinz heard the announcer declare that Beethoven's Ninth Symphony had just been completed under the direction of Wilhelm Furtwängler with Tibur de Machula as soloist.

Heinz saw from the distance the headwaiter talking on the telephone.

The news followed. The newscaster's voice announced new territorial gains in the West Caucasus while farther on the East Front the German forces had surrounded Soviet detachments near Lake Ilmen. There was heavy fighting in Egypt and Nigeria. John Bull was treating all citizens as slaves, forcing Nigerians to work in the tin mines.

The news ended and the radio offered some songs of Otto von Nicolai. After the food and beer Heinz's greatest desire was for bed. He looked forward eagerly to the moment when he could undress and slip between white sheets to sleep and sleep. But the fulfillment of this desire, he knew, was far away both in time and feasibility. He knew he could not risk registering in any hotel in the whole German Reich. Instead, he must continue to travel and to sleep in railroad stations or on trains. Perhaps he could make his bed outdoors in fields or woods, but not in a warm room inside a hotel or an inn. That comfort must wait.

Heinz called the waitress, but before he could pay for his meal a group of new customers arrived, and among them Heinz noticed a tall Gestapo officer in a black leather overcoat. The Gestapo man took off his cap, and Heinz noticed his red hair. It was Willi Bismar, Else's husband. The end, it appeared, was at hand.

XVII

November 1, 1942

Bismar moved directly to the table. "May I join you, Herr Hauptmann?"

Not waiting for an answer, Bismar sat down. Without taking off his overcoat he pulled out of his pocket a cigarette case from which he selected a gold-tipped Osiris, hit it carelessly against the closed case, and, using a gold Ronson, lighted it.

Bismar did not look at Heinz. With a glance he surveyed the people in the inn, then waved his large hand, summoning the waitress.

"What brands of cognac do you carry here?"

"Yes, right away, I will check it, please, Herr Sturmbannführer."

The good-natured smile had disappeared from her face. It was replaced by an expression of subservience and fear. Other people in the room watched Bismar with awe. Their conversation, full of joking and laughter, was reduced to a murmur. Bismar drew on his cigarette, observing the gold diamond ring on his finger. He spread a strong smell of Russian Leather cologne mixed with that of his expensive tobacco.

The waitress arrived and put a bottle of Asbach Uralt, a German brandy, on the table.

"I prefer to have the local Enzian. Bring us two glasses and take this . . . this stuff away!"

When the two glasses arrived, Bismar raised his. "It is always easier to begin a new acquaintance with a drink." He emptied his glass with one gulp. Heinz, as one hypnotized, did likewise. Then Bismar stood up, put a five mark note on the table, and, looking at Heinz, said, "Will you join me, Herr Hauptmann?"

In front of the inn was waiting a Mercedes with a driver in Gestapo uniform and another man in civilian clothes. No one spoke to Heinz as the car drove away.

From the window he glanced at the landscape and surmised that he was being transported to Munich. Would there be a chance to escape?

The car moved at some 150 kilometers per hour. As they entered Munich it slowed down. When they reached a building with two huge flags with the SS emblem, the car drove through an open gate guarded by uniformed SS men. As soon as they arrived Bismar disappeared. The man in civilian clothes led Heinz to a basement where he handed him over to a Gestapo man, apparently in charge of prisoners.

From the beginning of his confinement he was surprised by the nature of his treatment by his captors: it was extremely correct and to some degree polite, a contradiction of everything Heinz had heard about the way the Gestapo handled prisoners. He was certainly under very close supervision and there were always guards in his presence, but no one threatened him or tried to harm him.

The guard in charge of Heinz behaved more like a well-mannered porter in a first-class hotel than a Gestapo henchman. Heinz was first taken to a cell in the basement of the building and given the luxury of soap, towel, and enough warm water to wash himself comfortably. Then he was served a generous breakfast of a slice of ham, cheese, a slice of *Kommisbrot*, a *Kaisersemmel*, some butter, pinewood honey, and black currant jam.

Two uniformed Gestapo troopers came for him after he had finished his breakfast and accompanied him upstairs. After a hard knock at the door and a loud voice heard from inside calling "*Rein!*" the door was opened and Heinz was taken into the room. Instead of a chamber of horrors, as he had imagined, he found himself in what looked like a business executive's office with a large oak desk, a few comfortable chairs, oak cabinets, and a bookcase. The desk stood in front of a window now slightly ajar, and through it Heinz saw yellow horse chestnut trees.

There were two men in the room, both in uniform. The man behind the desk was in his early fifties with short gray hair. As Heinz entered he was finishing a telephone conversation which he did not conclude with the customary "Heil Hitler!" but with some other more personal greeting which he spoke in a voice so low that Heinz could not distinguish it. Both men rose. The man in front of the desk was Bismar.

Watching the two together it came to Heinz that he had seen both these men before. The scene returned to him: the field, where he had stood with the other hostages, the car driving up and, when it had stopped, the two men in the back standing up. These were those two men!

The man behind the desk introduced himself. "I am Obersturmbannführer Rudolf Malec and this is Sturmbannführer Bismar. You are Herr Heinz Hauptmann, is that correct?"

Malec looked carefully at Heinz and, when he did not not reply, added, "Will you sit down, please?" pointing to the other chair at his right.

"I know you are a nonsmoker," said Malec, "so I will not offer you a cigarette. However, if you would like, we can order some tea. Or perhaps you would like some real coffee."

Malec was casual, yet earnest. Heinz kept thinking that the whole scene might have taken place in some business headquarters, some office where two senior executives were conducting a lengthy interview for a management position.

"I do not want anything," Heinz said, sitting down.

Bismar, too, tried to appear relaxed, but there was an obvious tension in the behavior of both men. While Malec had no trouble controlling his voice, the nervous movements of his manicured hands and the frequent shifting of his legs betrayed him.

The moist air of the autumn morning penetrated the room and the sounds of children rushing to school could be heard: cheerful, happy voices. Someone in a neighboring building was practicing on a harpsichord, repeatedly playing the same Bach concerto movement. Knowing that beyond the window life was proceeding normally, Heinz felt more aware of his desperate situation than ever. As he faced his interrogators, a feeling of utter hopelessness engulfed him.

"Now, Herr Hauptmann," Malec continued, "I know your attitude toward us, and, as an experienced interrogator and also as a practical man, I suppose that you will tell us nothing. Am I correct?" Malec looked straight at Heinz.

"You are exactly right," Heinz said. "I am not going to tell you anything. You know I hate you. You are assassins, killers, merciless murderers." Heinz was unable to control his nerves and his hands trembled visibly.

"As you have no doubt noticed, Herr Hauptmann, you have not been badly treated here," interjected Bismar, who until now had remained silent, smoking one gold-tipped cigarette after another. "Nor do we have any intention of treating you badly." He paused long enough to light another cigarette. There was a silence in the room interrupted only by the distant music and a few passing cars on the street outside. "We are, Herr Hauptmann, as you know, in the middle of a great war," he continued. "Our survival as a nation is at stake. We are cleansing Europe of undesirable races. Other nations have done the same thing. We are merely following their example."

Then, smiling ironically at Heinz, he continued, "Some of these nations you perhaps call your friends—the English have always done this in their colonies, the Americans got rid of the Indians, and the Russians have killed millions of their own. We are just more methodical and better organized," Bismar concluded, pleased with himself. Then, after reflection, he added, "The good war is one which sanctifies everything, as Nietzsche said."

"None of those you mentioned killed children in gas chambers," Heinz retorted.

"We are thorough, as you know, and we have the right to bring new order because we are the victors," Bismar observed. "We must not only kill our enemies but our future enemies."

"Herr Hauptmann, I mentioned before that I understand your feelings and I know your attitude," Malec said. "And we did not bring you here for the purpose of changing either of them."

"So why don't you kill me now?" Heinz asked.

"I realize you must be tired," said Bismar to Heinz. "I will make this conversation as short as possible. Let me start in *medias res*—we want some information from you. We are realistic enough to realize that we will not be able to get this information by force. Consequently, in order to get it, we will offer you something in exchange."

"I will tell you nothing. There is nothing you can offer which will be of any value to me."

"There is always, in any situation, no matter how hopeless, something that a person may want very much," Malec said.

"I don't want to co-operate with you," Heinz said.

"Herr Hauptmann," Malec said, "we know that you are a native of Schlesien. We have learned that you are familiar with the area around the village Polansk. Some important documents were hidden in the area surrounding that village. You know, Herr Hauptmann, where they were hidden!

"Suppose," said Malec, "that these papers deal with real murderers of Poles, would you not give them to us? Suppose these papers unmask some very evil people?"

Heinz was exhausted but not physically. He was used to physical exertion. His fatigue came from knowing that he might not be able to escape in time to kill Hitler. All his hopes, his dreams, were destroyed. He did not fear anything now. He decided that he would not break, even if the price for his refusal to reveal the location of the papers was to be torture or death. He remembered the vow of silence he had made to his father.

Bismar rose and began pacing the room. "I spent one year in the United States," Bismar began. "In 1935 my father sent me there to study, not in a school, but just to meet people, to visit factories. It was interesting, fun even, but I did not learn very much, except . . ." Bismar stopped in front of Heinz, looking down with one sandy eyebrow raised imperceptibly. "Except, that no matter what, you can always make a 'deal,' an exchange, where both parties can benefit."

"We could arrest a Polish priest now under surveillance. I believe he visited you a few times." Bismar looked out the window. "He is a member of the Polish resistance and a spy for the Allies. By all international laws . . ."

"No, no, I won't. You will get nothing out of me."

The image of Father Sebastian in a concentration camp passed through Heinz's mind. Yet Heinz knew that Father Sebastian would never forgive him if he told his secret, even if it meant saving either of them.

Malec seemed displeased with the course the interrogation had taken. He looked at Bismar with distaste. As an experienced policeman and investigator, he knew human nature. He was aware that a man like Heinz would not make a deal. From his own experience he had learned that anyone has some weak point. The problem was to discover that weakness and then work on it. Malec had not yet been able to identify that weak point in Heinz.

"Herr Hauptmann, as part of my job, I have reviewed your dossier. I have learned many details of your life, your grades, your friendships, your travels. I have read all your examination papers, your German and English compositions."

Malec was now relaxed. He was doing a job, one he knew he was good at.

"I had to use an English-German dictionary to read your paper on Madison Grant. My own high school English is rusty and I have not had the opportunity to travel abroad. I was particularly keen to know the contents of this composition because that was one of the few cases in which you got a failing grade." Malec did not appear to fix his eyes on Heinz, yet not even the most minute change in Heinz's expression escaped this experienced interrogator.

Bismar sat silent and continued to smoke his cigarettes.

"I also read your best composition, your last exam. You had the choice among '*Iphigenie auf Tauris*' by Goethe 'and Its German Spirit,' then 'The Will to Live and the National Socialism,' and finally just simply 'A Landscape.' You chose the last."

Heinz wondered what all this talk was about. He tried to interrupt Malec, who with a hand motioned him to be silent.

"You wrote an essay about the river, the fields, the dark forest, the flowers. I liked the way you wrote it, particularly your reference to folklore. I liked the myth about the nymph having the right to turn a loved one into a cornflower. Would you not want to revisit that landscape?"

The idea had occurred to Heinz. If he were taken back to Polansk, maybe he could escape!

Malec smiled. "Would you?"

"Yes," replied Heinz.

Malec looked at Bismar. "Herr Sturmbannführer and I will take a trip to Polansk. Will you please return to Herr Hauptmann his personal effects?"

Heinz did not trust him. He knew what Malec was after. Yet Heinz was also aware that there would be no chance to escape from a well-guarded Gestapo headquarters. The only hope would be to flee while they were under way or in Polansk, where he knew every spot in the woods and every trail in the radius of several kilometers of Polansk.

XVIII

November 2, 1942

Bismar walked with Heinz to the basement. He saw to it that the guard returned to Heinz all his belongings, his watch, ration coupons, food, flashlight, but not his documents. Then Bismar pulled out from his pocket a dried four-leaf clover.

"I kept it to preserve it," Bismar said. "I guess you are collecting those. They are supposed to bring good luck. Well, you may need it, Herr Hauptmann."

Heinz wanted to tell Bismar, "You may need it, too, you brute," but controlled his urge and just nodded his head.

In about an hour they were ready to leave. A black Mercedes sedan with a chauffeur in Gestapo uniform waited in the middle of the court. At the gate the guards, who knew both Bismar and Malec, nevertheless checked everybody's documents: permits to leave the Gestapo headquarters and identification papers. One guard came close to compare the photographs with the faces of the men. When the guard was returning his papers to him, Heinz noticed that two fingers of his left hand were missing. He looked up to see a tall, broad-shouldered man in his late thirties.

The day continued to be clear and Heinz looked out of the window at the streets of Munich. He remembered his vacation there with Andreas, his dreams and hopes.

They passed a sign indicating the approach to the autobahn. Suddenly a Gestapo courier on a motorcycle caught up with their car and stopped it. The driver lowered the window.

"A message for Obersturmbannführer Malec," the driver of the motorcycle shouted. Malec got out of the car, walked up to the cyclist, took from him a sealed envelope, opened it, and read the message. Heinz saw his hands shaking. The motorcyclist stood by. After Malec had finished reading, he folded the paper carefully and put it into his breast pocket; he spoke briefly to the man on the motorcycle, who immediately turned his vehicle and departed. Then Malec approached the car.

He looked at Bismar, who quickly got out of the car. As they walked away, Heinz watched their silhouettes move down the street. He could see they were engaged in animated conversation. When they returned Heinz noticed that Bismar's face, usually reddish, had turned the color of ashes. Malec's face was grave. They stopped some ten meters away from the car and stood silently for about ten more minutes, until another Gestapo Mercedes arrived; Bismar saluted Malec, clicking his heels, and entered the newly arrived car.

Heinz looked at the side mirror and saw there the face of the driver. The man smiled with satisfaction.

Malec took his seat next to Heinz in the back of the car and the journey continued. The car took the autobahn, where they passed many military vehicles, ambulances, and an occasional nonmilitary car with the swastika emblem on the small flag.

The road ran smoothly across a plain; about an hour later it began to wind around low hills. Heinz noticed a series of fields covered with hops supported by tall wooden structures.

"Best hops in the world are grown in this area," Malec said, seeing Heinz's interest.

"Where I lived, no such luck, sandy soil . . . nothing but potatoes." Malec was observing Heinz, who did not want to give Malec reasons for more comments and focused his eyes on the ceiling of the car.

"Family of nine kids, a small farm. All of us had to work on the farm in addition to going to school. I used to look forward to the end of the vacations. Then we used to get two weeks of *Kartoffelferien*, potato vacation, so we could help to dig them out. Our food for the whole year was potatoes—with sour cream, with lard, with salt, or in dumplings, home fried, boiled with dill. I guess three hundred varieties." Malec looked again at the landscape.

"You know, Herr Hauptmann, the farm on which I was born and grew up is only some fifty kilometers from your native village." Not expecting any comments from Heinz, Malec continued, "The soil on your farm is better. You used to grow wheat mostly?"

"Wheat and some barley," Heinz said, regretting to be drawn into a conversation with Malec.

"There were some beets and turnips too?"

"Yes turnips and beets."

"Did you help your father, Herr Hauptmann?"

Heinz turned his head. "No."

"I thought so, but I had to work. What did you want to become, I mean had the war not occurred? What profession?"

"I guess an officer, cavalry, uhlan."

"You know, that was my dream and desire also when I was your age. I even applied. I knew how to ride a horse. This was 1910. All of us recruits had to mount a horse. I still remember that day. We were sitting on horses, all the recruits I mean. The Herr Rittmeister von Lippitz arrived on his white Arabian horse. A sergeant with a notebook followed him. Von Lippitz looked at each of us through his gold-rimmed monocle and made the decision, yes or no."

The hills in their field of vision were covered now with woods. The yellow leaves still reflected the autumn sunshine.

"When he stopped in front of me, he laughed. All the other recruits laughed too. Then in a loud voice, which could be heard by everyone, he said, 'This sack of potatoes on a horse? Oh no, sir, not in my regiment.' Well, that was the end of my dream and desire for the cavalry."

Heinz wondered why Malec was telling him about his life. He suspected that Malec was trying to establish a rapport so that Heinz would tell him where his father had hidden the papers. "Do not treat me like a boy, Herr Malec," he said curtly. They drove on in silence.

Most of the way, both Malec and Heinz remained silent. Slowly fatigue overtook Heinz and he fell asleep, both troubled and profound.

It was dark when they arrived at their destination, a Baroque building situated in the middle of a large park. Despite its location far away from the main road or any town, the rules of complete blackout applied. There was no light visible from outside.

As soon as they entered a large vestibule lighted by a chandelier with hundreds of lights, Heinz thought the place must be a castle. Most of the men who were there wore the uniform of the SS; others were SS men temporarily wearing civilian clothes and displaying the SS emblem in their lapels.

Malec and Heinz were assigned a suite, two bedrooms divided by a large sitting room decorated in Louis XVI style. The driver was assigned a different kind of accommodation and a few minutes after their arrival he disappeared.

They ate in a spacious dining room. There was a good choice of food, including a variety of exotic dishes, like venison, pheasant, and partridges. The menu did not indicate prices or the ration coupon requirements.

During the dinner Malec explained to Heinz that the castle had been built as a hunting lodge by the Duke of Saxony and King of Poland, August the Strong. In the morning they would take a tour. The king's bedroom had on one huge wall approximately twenty portraits of Polish ladies, mistresses of the king, and another wall was decorated by an equal number of portraits of English ladies, also mistresses of the king. Malec treated Heinz like a guest who deserved courtesy, and he avoided in his conversation any subject which would have reminded Heinz of his real status.

After the dinner they retired to their own living room. On the table stood a bottle of Asbach Uralt and two glasses. They sat down and Malec poured the liquor: "You must be wondering why we stopped here at this unusual place." Malec sipped the brandy. "The answer is a very simple one. It is much better than Gestapo regional headquarters in Dresden. I am bringing up that subject to indicate that this place, which serves as an SS meeting ground and as a recreation center, is as well guarded as the headquarters." The thick wall protected them from any noise or sound. One heard only the ticking of an eighteenth-century brass clock on a side table. Malec opened the buttons of his uniform tunic. In the bright light of the chandelier his face looked tired, wrinkled, and square.

"I like this kind of luxury, at least once in a while." He took another sip from his glass and with a gesture encouraged Heinz to join him. Heinz obeyed. He had the feeling that Malec wanted to speak to him about something important. He would not have kept Heinz up for the evening to talk about banalities. Yet Malec continued to talk about his life, farms, studies, police work. Heinz concentrated on planning an escape and hardly listened to Malec. It was getting late; they had finished a major portion of their bottle. Malec was sitting now with his boots off, sipping from his glass with increasing frequency, when he said:

"I know you have wondered since we have arrived here why I am wasting my time and yours, right?" Malec did not wait for Heinz to answer this question. "I was wondering why myself. Well, one of the explanations may be guilt. I don't know."

Heinz was stunned by that confession. Another ploy to make him reveal where the papers were hidden?

"You are now young. You do not understand why a Gestapo officer would say such a thing. Well, I will tell you—it is difficult to justify in one's own mind everything that happens." Malec did not look at Heinz. He finished the brandy with one gulp, then poured another one. He rose and began pacing. "One does hope that the end justifies the means . . . that eventually we will live in a better world."

He stopped in front of a window and kept looking at the curtain that covered the glass of the window as if the piece of material were transparent.

"We are all living in the time of a hurricane, a storm of dreadful proportions. I don't know how and why this storm got unleashed; nobody knows. I did not have anything to do with unleashing those dark forces. I know I am part of it. . . . Perhaps I play a big part in it. But I am a professional, I have a high stake in this business." Malec returned to pacing. He stopped in front of Heinz.

"I don't know whether I will survive, but I am trying. That must be your objective too. Do you understand me?"

Malec returned to his armchair, raised the glass, but placed it back on the table without drinking from it.

"If I were you, I would get a job on a farm in Germany, somewhere in the mountains. You could eat there better than most of us living in towns. You could stay far away from the bombs or other dangers."

"But I am not a farmer," Heinz said.

"You seem to like nature," Malec said. "You are fond of trees. Your favorite is the . . . ? I forgot what . . . ?"

"The oak, I think I wrote."

"I had the impression you were also fond of . . . the name escapes me. All these drinks . . . honeybee's choice?"

"I don't remember."

"Oh yes, the linden tree. I think in your essay you mentioned the legend about this tree. It is revered as a tree of immortality in your country and in the Tyrol it is a haunt of dragons and dwarfs." Malec focused his eyes on Heinz.

"Oh yes, I wrote about it because a friend of mine makes tea from the blossoms. I drink it very often."

"On our farm there is a linden tree," Malec said. "For a poor farmer it is a plague."

"But why?" Heinz asked.

"It has shallow roots," Malec said. "Nothing will grow around it for six, eight, or more meters. Did you ever try to dig under a linden tree?" Malec again focused his eyes on Heinz, who blushed. Not waiting for his answer, Malec continued, "Under an oak tree you could dig a hole only centimeters away from its trunk, but not a linden tree."

Malec stood up. "I guess we better catch some sleep. Good night." He strode toward his room. "Do you know what tree survives the worst storms? The willow. The oaks are the first to fall, but the willow bends and survives. You could do a little bending. Remember what I told you before. The key is to survive, and then in such a way that you could live with your conscience. You could do that. Good night again."

Heinz had a troubled sleep and he woke up when it was still dark. He heard voices and footsteps in the living room. Among those speaking he heard Malec. The doors opened and closed, and then there was silence again.

When Heinz got up and entered the living room, he was surprised to see the driver of the car sitting in the armchair that Malec had occupied before. The driver, the same age as Heinz, with sandy hair and a sandy mustache, stood up.

"I am glad to see you, Herr Hauptmann. We must leave soon."

"But the Obersturmbannführer . . . ?"

"Herr Obersturmbannführer had to leave . . . unexpectedly. He will meet us in Polansk tonight."

When Heinz approached the car, he saw another Gestapo man sitting in the front next to the driver's seat. The chauffeur who had picked Heinz up in his room sat down next to him. They proceeded in silence. When the car had to make a left turn, the driver signaled with his left hand, the one with the missing fingers, and Heinz realized that the man at the wheel was the same Gestapo guard who had cleared their car for departure from the headquarters in Munich.

The car crossed the Elbe River and entered Dresden. The driver stopped in front of an inn, disappeared for a moment, and came out with another man. Heinz recognized immediately the driver's companion: he was the director of the Nyphelheimer Oberschule, Harimann.

XIX

November 3, 1942

On the morning of November 3, Father Sebastian got up early. He dressed in flannel trousers and a tweed jacket of the same color. He put on a loden overcoat and a green felt Tyrol hat. He packed a small valise in which he put a compass, a meter to measure the distance, a flashlight, and a map. From a hiding place in the wall, he pulled out money and a passport made out to the name of Georg Schultz, a Volksdeutsche. He also took a *Grenzschein* authorizing him to cross the border from General Gouvernement to the Third Reich, only less than ten kilometers away from where he lived. Father Sebastian also packed enough food for a stay of three days.

On the way to the railroad station, Father Sebastian stopped at Jozef's, the gardener, where he bought a spade, which he wrapped so that it looked more like a viola d'amore than a spade. Polansk was only some seventy kilometers away, but it took Father Sebastian the full day to reach it. He had to take a train, then change twice, take a bus, and walk for the last ten kilometers. When he arrived in Polansk, it was dark already.

On his way to the beet field he had to pass the Leski house, where he had visited the family so often before the war.

Father Sebastian arrived at the empty space where Heinz's home had stood. He recognized the garden despite the changes of time, and the trees, which had grown since he saw them last.

The garden where Heinz had played as a child was now the village public park. Father Sebastian approached the place where the house had stood. With the ground leveled and grass sown over the spot, he felt as if he were standing at a grave. The living house with its memories was now only a field of grass. He searched for some tangible piece of the past until he found under the tangled roots of a barren lilac a piece of the broken leg of the piano Pani Leski had played. He recognized the rotted, partly burned piece of wood by the wheel still attached to it. The only memento of the sounds of laughter, singing, and music.

With sadness he continued to walk toward the beet field. He had walked often with Heinz, then Adam, in the fields of the Leski farm and knew well the linden tree where Heinz's father had buried the box with the documents. Father Sebastian did not rush to start digging. He was afraid to arouse suspicion. It was dark, but he wanted to start digging late enough not to be met by a farmer returning from a visit. For a few hours he sat several yards from the road behind some bushes and ate the bread and boiled eggs he had brought along.

Only around midnight did he move toward the linden tree. He took out his compass, flashlight, and meter and measured carefully the distance: ten meters north of the tree. Then he unwrapped the spade and began to dig.

Father Sebastian's spade grated against the hard soil. The top few inches of the earth were frozen and it took him a good five minutes to reach the softer soil below the frost line. The night was cold, windy, and dark, and, unaccustomed to digging, Father Sebastian made only slow progress. The first hole he dug turned out to be too small to reach the proper depth and to enlarge it he had to fight the frozen top soil again and again. It took him an hour to reach the proper depth. But there was no sign of the metal box. He returned to the tree and measured the distance once more, checking the direction by the compass. His calculations proved his initial estimate to be correct.

Father Sebastian spent another hour enlarging the hole to the right; then he worked to the left. His watch showed it was three o'clock in the morning. He was tired, hungry, and thirsty, but he knew he had to finish the job within the next few hours. He returned to the center and dug in the direction of the tree. By now his fingers were bleeding and his right shoe damaged so that his work proceeded slowly. It was after six o'clock in the morning when his spade hit hard on a metal object. It was the box.

With shaking hands he pulled it from the ground, then crawled out of the hole with his prize. With the help of the spade he opened the box and pulled out the papers, which were wrapped in a moisture resistant sheet. He took his flashlight, unwrapped the cover, and with trembling hands opened the top folder. In the silence, broken only by the distant barking of a dog, Father Sebastian could hear the beat of his own heart. He was holding in his hands the documents which had caused many deaths. The first document was typed, double spaced. The first few pages contained statements familiar to him. They were nothing more than the familiar Nazi doctrines. The language was typical: obscure, imprecise, larded with flowery expressions and inconsequential logic.

Father Sebastian was disappointed; there was nothing of consequence. It was like reading an old, long-accepted textbook. Then he began to discern some differences. None of them were significant disagreements with the core of the Nazi doctrine but they provided for more radical applications and detailed the consequences.

The document outlined the organization of the Nazi society and its position on non-Nordic races: the complete *Ausradierung* of the Slavonic nations with speedy elimination of the populations. The program stipulated the details of the organization, including a time schedule and procedures for its implementation, even down to the disposition of property confiscated and the settlement of the Germans in the conquered areas. It stipulated a Nazi society organized in camps, with separate camps for the women, who would bear and rear children, and for the men, who would work, conduct wars, and kill. Reading would be limited to practical books; all others would be banned, except to a select group of scientists and specially trained leaders.

In this society there would be no freedom of action or thought. And, of course, there would be no love and no God, thought Father Sebastian as he read.

The contents of the second folder surprised him. This document attacked Adolf Hitler as a slow and ineffective leader, unable to accomplish the desired reforms. It carefully outlined plans to eliminate him through an organized assassination and proposed the creation of a new Fourth Reich under the leadership of Heinrich Himmler, with the support of the Gestapo under the direction of—Father Sebastian blinked in amazement—Otto Harimann. The papers were dated early in 1939. He had not believed that there could be worse murderers and more evil men than Adolf Hitler. Now he wondered.

With frozen fingers, bloody now from digging, he reached for the third folder. After the others it really didn't matter to him what this one contained, but he felt compelled to finish reading.

The last folder contained a number of letters in English to which were attached the German translations and copies of the replies in German. All the letters in English came from New York and were dated 1937, 1938, and the first half of 1939.

One of the early letters began, "With great sorrow we inform you that Mr. Grant passed away. His thoughts and his work will contribute to our future more than that of any other man in history."

It was getting lighter and Father Sebastian did not need to use the flashlight to see. The one dated April 10, 1939, from New York caught his eye:

> Adolf Hitler is not acceptable to us for the following reasons:

a) It is not clear to us whether he has 100% Aryan blood. As you know there are serious doubts on this subject.
b) We find his social doctrines and programs almost communist. These must be scrapped. Himmler, with his emphasis on purity of the Aryan blood defined as Germanic and Anglo, would be our choice for the right leader in your country who we would work with as your representative. We must insist on total elimination of Negroes, Jews, Slavs and other non-Anglo-Germanic races.

Father Sebastian knew that his time was limited. Yet he quickly started to read another letter, the last one in that part of the folder. This letter also came from New York and was dated June 16, 1939:

Our survey indicates that a substantial majority will be on our side. We should expect from you:

1) A speedy clean-up in your country and the future territories under your domination of the racially undesirable peoples, demonstrating—
   a) That this can be done
   b) The time required for such actions
2) Military training of your elite troops which would participate with our units to take over the government of the United States
3) Elimination of Adolf Hitler

The last action would constitute for us a signal to take over our government within a period of six months.

The division of the occupation will be as follows: Germany would control Europe less British Isles, Ireland, and Iceland

Africa

Asia: only the parts currently under Soviet domination. The rest of the world would be considered as the American sphere of interest.

Father Sebastian stopped reading. Thank God that all this did not come true. Now America was in the war against the Nazis.

Father Sebastian was tired and cold. He arranged the papers in a pile, then he pulled out a match and lighted them. The fire did not take at first, but after the third try the papers began to burn. He waited until the last scrap of papers turned to ashes, then he walked slowly toward the road.

The new day was cold and patches of fog covered the fields and the road. At the moment Father Sebastian forgot the cold and the hunger. Some sentences from the documents continued to hit him: "complete *Ausradierung* of the Slavonic nations . . . purity of Aryan blood . . . total elimination of Negroes, Jews, Slavs. . . . More evil than Hitler, it would be worse than now, Father Sebastian thought.

A truck loaded with coal passed him and stopped only several meters from him. The driver came out and walked toward him. Despite the overalls and a face covered by coal dust, Father Sebastian recognized him; the blue eyes contrasted with the almost black skin. It was Stefan Wirski, his colleague in the Underground.

"No time for explanations," Stefan said. "Did you burn the papers?"

Father Sebastian nodded. "Good," Stefan said. "Very good."

The next day Stefan came to Father Sebastian's house. Wirski was a small, sturdily built man of fifty. He had blond hair that was turning to gray now, and blue eyes that indicated a fierce intensity. They were brave eyes that spoke of a quiet heroism, a courage that knew no limits, and a passion that could not be stilled. His wife had been murdered by the Nazis, and his brother was now in a concentration camp. He would not rest until his brother was freed and his wife avenged. Here in one man was the strength of Poland.

Lilka had called and reported Heinz's sudden disappearance. Father Sebastian had asked Wirski to come see him because he needed his help to find Heinz.

From the moment Wirski arrived it was clear that something

was bothering him. Father Sebastian offered him a cup of tea, which he declined, pacing nervously around the room.

"Is there something wrong, Stefan?"

"Yes, Father, there is," he said, looking directly into the priest's eyes. "The boy, Leski, tried to assassinate Hitler. The Gestapo is onto him. He won't last long. I'm sorry."

Father Sebastian was shocked. Suddenly he realized that Heinz's insistence on going back to school must be connected to this. He thought to ask Wirski how he knew this, but Stefan could see the question forming in his mind and volunteered the information.

"He tried to kill Hitler with a crossbow, and very nearly succeeded," he said.

"Do they know his real identity?" he asked. "They'll torture him if they think he knows where the Komm papers are."

"They know he is Adam Leski. One of the boys at the school, Andreas Wendel, is working for the Gestapo. I'm afraid our young friend is not the most careful assassin. When he came back to Poland, the Gestapo knew that he was Leski. They had him followed."

"Why haven't they arrested him?" Father Sebastian asked.

"They suspect that he's in league with the Himmler faction within the Party, and they're hoping he'll lead them to the others involved. He hasn't got a chance, Father. They'll arrest him within a few days," Wirski said, putting his hand gently on the old priest's shoulder.

"We've got to find him, Stefan. The boy is so important to me. Maybe . . ." Father Sebastian was speaking frantically as his eyes wandered past Wirski out a small window through which the morning sun came. He was filled with despair, and a memory of a churchyard and the Polish men who died with Heinz's father.

"Father, there is no chance. The boy is doomed," Stefan said. His appraisal was harsh but realistic. He'd seen dozens of men die, and knew that the effort of the Underground must not be wasted. When Father Sebastian looked at him, he saw Wirski's sadness turning into anger.

"I'm tired of children who know nothing of war," Wirski said.

"I won't chase all over for a boy who gave himself over to this obsession. He could have stayed here and worked for the Underground. Instead, he's a useless assassin, and will soon be a dead assassin."

He spoke passionately and, when he finished, looked with pity at Father Sebastian. For a moment there was a profound silence and his anger filled the air and slowly dissipated. A tension built between the two men.

Stefan turned to Father Sebastian. "I'm sorry, Father. He's a brave boy. It's just that . . ."

Father Sebastian interrupted him and said, "I know, Stefan, everything you said is true. But, please, won't you help me find him? I love that boy."

"Of course I will, Father. Poland needs all her sons," he said. "It's best to wait until dark. I'll contact you this evening."

"Thank you," Father Sebastian said, investing those words with all the admiration he could. Stefan quietly slipped out of the room and into the morning light.

XX

November 4, 1942

Harimann entered the car and greeted Heinz with a smile. "This is an unexpected pleasure, Herr Hauptmann," he said, shaking Heinz's hand. He appeared to be in good spirits. He wore a brown tweed jacket and flannel trousers of the same color. His sparse grayish hair was kept in place by an overgenerous application of brilliantine. The white collar of his shirt looked as if it had come only seconds ago from the laundry.

"I hope, Herr Hauptmann, that you will not mind the company of your, shall we say, educator." Harimann laughed briefly. "Dresden happens to be my home town. I was born here." Harimann proved his knowledge of the town by pointing out to Heinz the *Hofkirche*, *Frauenkirche*, *Zwinger*, and other buildings of historical interest. He even asked the driver to make a number of detours to show Heinz these monuments.

It was almost noon when they left Dresden to continue their

journey east. About two hours later Harimann asked the driver to stop in front of an inn, Zur Krone, near a town called Bautzen. According to Harimann, the inn had some literary significance. Here, according to some legend, Goethe had conceived the idea for his major work, *Faust*. The inn was furnished with oak tables and chairs in the provincial style of Saxony and could have been two hundred years old by the appearance of the huge oak cupboards and closets. On the window sills red geraniums in bloom were standing. By some tacit agreement the party separated; Harimann and Heinz took the table in one corner near the window, the two Gestapo men sat near the exit.

After Heinz and Harimann had ordered food, Heinz could check his curiosity no longer. He fired questions at Harimann.

"Are we going to Polansk? Are we going to meet Malec there? Why were you chosen to accompany me?"

Heinz welcomed Harimann's involvement. He hoped that it would be easier to escape from Harimann's supervision than from Malec's.

"You want to know everything at one time," Harimann said, looking out of the window. "I promise you, in due course your questions will be answered, plus many more, even those you have not asked."

The morning, sunny and bright, turned now to a dark autumn day and the first drops of rain began hitting the window.

"Well anyway, I don't think that you will meet Malec in Polansk or anywhere else." He turned toward Heinz and focused his eyes through his horn-rimmed glasses on Heinz's face. "Malec is now on the way to Wolfsschanze, the Führer's headquarters in East Prussia."

"So the Führer will not come to Munich?" Heinz asked.

"Oh no, my boy, Malec is there to arrange the security for this trip. He is a very clever policeman. He has the reputation of being number one in Europe. Would you agree?"

A freckle-faced, middle-aged waitress brought the food. In silence Harimann cut a small piece of sausage and swallowed it with a gulp of water.

"The Oberschule, Herr Hauptmann, takes care of our students. . . . Even if they are in trouble with the police. Our responsibility is greater for those of our students who have lost their parents."

Harimann drank another glass of water. "In such cases I assume also the duties of students' parents."

"I have not committed a . . ." Heinz said. "I did not do anything," he corrected himself.

Harimann stopped eating, wiped his glasses with his handkerchief, put them on again. "I know it, Herr Hauptmann. This is why I am with you now."

"So am I free now?"

"You will be returning to school with me, Herr Hauptmann."

"But when?" Heinz hoped that it would not be difficult to escape from school, go from there to Munich, find a tunnel north of it and jump on the train. He didn't trust Harimann. This sudden turn of good fortune made him suspicious.

"I have some business in this part of Germany," Harimann said. "Today is Wednesday, the fourth. We should be in the school by this weekend."

Heinz began to plan how he could escape. He would have to escape before the weekend to kill the Führer.

"I will be away for a day or so. In the meantime you will remain in the custody of these two young men. I have rented a room for the three of you in this place. You will be quite comfortable."

After lunch Heinz moved into a large room with three beds.

For the next twenty-four hours he was never alone. One or the other of his guards was with him. Meals were served in the room. On the evening of the following day Harimann returned, told Heinz that all of them would be leaving the next morning, and invited one of the men to his room next door.

When they were ready to leave, Heinz was surprised to learn that the two guards were to travel in a separate car and that he would be driving alone with Harimann. It was a cloudy morning with occasional showers. Harimann had to drive slowly, concentrating all his attention on the road. Heinz noticed that Harimann took the road to Leipzig, a city north of Dresden, which was in the opposite direction from Munich and the Oberschule.

They had been driving for about ten minutes when Harimann broke the awkward silence.

"Herr Hauptmann, I share your desire to see Hitler dead," he said bluntly. Heinz said nothing, and tried not to show his surprise. Harimann kept his eyes fixed on the road ahead of him.

"He murdered my parents, too, and I have no intention of standing in the way of your plan," he said. "In fact, I can help you. I know the precise route and schedule of the Führer's train."

Heinz did not believe Harimann's story about his parents being killed by the Nazis; he knew now that Harimann was part of Piersohn's group. He did not care what Harimann's reasons were. He only knew they had a common goal.

"Herr Hauptmann, or should I say Leski, if you tell me where the Komm papers are, I am prepared to 'arrange' an escape for you," he said, reaching into his inside pocket and pulling out a small revolver, which he aimed casually at Heinz.

It might give him enough time to get to Hitler, Heinz thought.

"The papers are buried ten meters due north of the linden tree in the beet field on my family's farm," he said quickly. "I'm sure you know where that is, in Polansk."

Harimann slowed down and talked matter-of-factly, his eyes still trained on the road ahead. "At midnight, or shortly thereafter, the train will pass through a station called Sterbfritz, located between Fulda and Gemünden. It's located in a valley between two tunnels. From the overpass to the north of the station you can jump on the train. Hitler is in the seventh or eighth car, the one numbered 10215." He slowed down, pulled off the road, and handed Heinz the gun as he motioned him out of the car. "Good luck," he said.

Heinz grabbed his rucksack and, sticking the gun in it, ran for the woods that lined the road. He looked back quickly toward Harimann, who had already driven off down the road to announce the prisoner's escape and organize a manhunt.

XXI

November 5, 1942

Father Sebastian arrived at two in the afternoon in Katowice and half an hour later knocked at the door of the apartment at which Stefan had agreed to meet him. A young woman in her late twenties with thick blond braids opened the door and, without asking any questions, invited him inside.

"I recognize you, Father," she said. "I attended a mass celebrated by you when you were here in Katowice."

They entered a small living room where two preschool-age children were playing.

"My name is Kasia," she continued. "May I offer you . . ."

"No, thank you," Father Sebastian said and looked at Kasia.

"One of our members just delivered this message for you." She lifted a pot of red geraniums, and from under the saucer took an envelope. She handed it over to Father Sebastian. The envelope contained ration coupons for travelers valid in the area of the whole Third Reich, 1,000 marks, and a note:

"Take the train to Vienna at eight this evening, then to Munich. Meet me on Saturday, the seventh, Schloss Nymphenburg, in Munich, between two and three in the afternoon." It was signed by Stefan.

Kasia was separating the two boys, who were fighting over a ball. Father Sebastian tore up the note in small pieces and Kasia led him to the kitchen, where he threw them into the fire. She invited him to dinner, but he declined. Father Sebastian was concerned that his presence might endanger Kasia. He preferred to walk about the town or dine at a restaurant while waiting for the train.

Father Sebastian followed his instructions, proceeding on the journey and arriving in Munich the evening before his meeting. He rented a room in Stuttgarter Hof but could not fall asleep. He worried about Heinz. He was afraid that Heinz would be killed trying to kill Hitler. He hoped Stefan had found him.

The next morning he walked to the Liebfrauenkirche, the main church in Munich, attended a mass, and prayed for Heinz's safety.

After lunch he took a streetcar to the park around the Schloss Nymphenburg, a Baroque structure surrounded by well-trimmed bushes. He admired Stefan for selecting this place for their rendezvous. This was the least likely place for the police to watch them.

There was a group of tourists gathering for a guided tour of the château. One visitor, in a gabardine overcoat and a felt Borsolino hat, detached himself from the group and walked toward Father Sebastian. Only when the stranger was a few meters away did Father Sebastian recognize him as Stefan Wirski.

After they strolled a few hundred meters away from the crowds, Stefan said, "We have made progress. We know the general area where we might find Heinz."

"Is it far from here?" Father Sebastian asked.

"Somewhere north of Würzburg," Wirski said. "We have discovered that the director of the Oberschule, Harimann, is Himmler's crony," Stefan said. "It is now likely that Harimann's boss plans a small change in the leadership of the Reich. In his favor, of course."

It was a sunny autumn day, and most of the leaves, now gold or yellow, were still on the trees. They reached the end of the park, turned around, and ambled back toward the Schloss.

"How did you discover that Heinz was in that area?" Father Sebastian asked.

Wirski smiled. "Some simple work, a telephone tap. Herr Harimann got a call from Gemünden from a Herr Piersohn."

Father Sebastian remembered the papers and the mention of Harimann's name.

"Gemünden happens to be located on the main railroad line—north-south," Stefan said.

"But will Herr Piersohn, when we find him, give us the information?" Father Sebastian asked. "Will he tell us where Heinz is? We have so little time."

Wirski had somehow commandeered a car and he seemed to be familiar with German roads and did not need any direction to Gemünden, a small town which they reached by nine that evening. There seemed to be only one restaurant open, an establishment called Zum Goldenen Baum.

"How do we recognize him?" Father Sebastian asked as they were standing in front of the entrance.

"We have his description," Stefan said. "He's easy to spot—big and fat, gray mustache."

Two soldiers left the Zum Goldenen Baum, and through the opened doors they saw a big fat man sitting inside.

They entered the restaurant. Piersohn sat alone at the table and drank beer. Four other customers sat at another table: two young soldiers with their girls.

The two of them approached Piersohn's table and Stefan asked in German, "May we join you?"

Piersohn beamed. He nodded his head and repeated a few times, "*Bitte, bitte sehr, meine Herren!*" He was not surprised. In small towns it is usual to come to a restaurant with empty tables and to sit down at one partly occupied.

"The bar is closed," the owner of the establishment shouted.

"That's all right," Father Sebastian responded. Turning to Piersohn, he said, "We came here to see you, Herr Piersohn. We would like to discuss a private matter."

"How can I help you?" Piersohn said and took a gulp from his stein. He scrutinized each of them.

"We would rather discuss it in private," Father Sebastian added.

"We are friends," Stefan said, "of a friend of yours. If you don't mind, we would prefer to talk about him. Well, in your room, perhaps?"

"I understand," Piersohn said. "*Herr Ober!* The check, please."

Piersohn carefully put on his galoshes, his gray homburg, and peccary gloves. Then from a rack he picked up his umbrella and walked out. The others followed him. Outside they walked in silence.

The Hotel Zum Stern seemed to be empty and they strode up the stairs to the second-floor room without seeing anyone.

Piersohn's room was large, with a bed, a sofa, a table, and two chairs. After they had taken their coats off and sat down, Wirski and Piersohn at the table and Father Sebastian on the sofa, Piersohn asked:

"What can I do for you?"

"Our names," Father Sebastian began, "will tell you very little. But we have, all of us here in this room, one thing in common. We are all friends of Heinz Hauptmann."

"Oh, how nice," Piersohn exclaimed in English. "I bid you most cordial and hearty welcome."

"Herr Piersohn," Wirski said, "we need a favor from you."

"I cannot conceive," Piersohn said, "a greater honor and say how glad I am to render it, sir."

"We must rush," Wirski said.

The hotel seemed to be empty. There were no noises to be heard. Only the rain hitting the window glass broke the silence when no one was speaking.

"I will hurry," Piersohn said, "like a great express train, roaring, flashing, dashing headlong."

The visitors exchanged glances. . . . Father Sebastian's tweed jacket was crumpled, he was tired and sleepy. Stefan also seemed exhausted, but Piersohn seemed to enjoy himself in the company of these men. He liked their attention.

"We need, Mr. Piersohn," Wirski said, "to find Heinz. Will you help us?"

Piersohn took out of his side pocket the gold-plated cigar cutter and used it, lighted his cigar, and turned to Wirski.

"Please do not think," Piersohn said, "that I am asking out of mere curiosity, but why do you endeavor to find this young man?"

"We have our reasons," Wirski said. "We are willing to compensate you for this information."

"I should forfeit my own self-respect and I should be false to my own manhood if I would consider discussing this subject. Forgive me if I seem disobliging."

"I am sorry, Herr Piersohn," Wirski said. "We have no time to waste. I can offer you twenty-five thousand marks. Just name the place."

The mention of the amount shook Piersohn. His monocle fell from his right eye and hit the table. He remained silent, searching for the appropriate phrase.

"I am at a loss for adequate expression," Piersohn said. "I have been touched by your large generosity, but I do not need to remind you that if I report you special . . ."

"Well, Herr Piersohn?" Wirski took out of his brief case the bills and put them on the table in front of Piersohn.

Piersohn put back the monocle and looked at the money. The drops of perspiration appeared on his forehead.

"Yes, Herr Piersohn?" Wirski began to withdraw the money into his brief case.

"Yes, sir, I shall yield to the ingratiating mood of the day. I am indebted for the honor and . . ."

"Where is he, Herr Piersohn?" Wirski asked.

"I feel like an iridescent bubble floating on a foul stream of these times," Piersohn said self-indulgently, fingering the money greedily.

"Where? Where is he?" Wirski asked.

"He is in Sterbfritz. A small . . ."

"I know where the place is."

"Do you know where he might be in Sterbfritz?"

"No, sir, I deem to . . ."

"We must hurry. Now, Piersohn, let me tell you that if you have lied to us or if you inform on us, you will be killed."

Without waiting for any comment they rushed to the car.

Father Sebastian looked at his watch. It was eleven o'clock in the evening.

When Wirski sat down behind the wheel he said, "Another five minutes of listening to Mr. Piersohn and I would have vomited. We will have to make a big detour. That place can be reached only by a dirt road from Steinau."

They reached Sterbfritz in an hour and a half. After parking the car a few hundred meters away from the railroad station, they decided that Father Sebastian should walk north along the train tracks, Stefan should follow the tracks south. They planned to meet in an hour at the same spot near the parked car.

They met again precisely as agreed.

"I could not walk along the tracks," Father Sebastian said. "There are uniformed men. This proves that the Führer's train has not passed here yet."

"Did you try," Wirski asked, "to go parallel to the tracks?"

"As long as the time allowed me," Father Sebastian said. "Tough going. Dense bushes, boysenberries, and raspberries."

"The tunnel to the south of the station," Stefan said, "starts only a few hundred meters from here. There was no problem in reaching it. I checked on the area above the tunnel—also bushes. But I will tell you, I have never been in a place quite like that. There is fog, you cannot see for more than a meter. And it is drizzling." He turned around to check whether they were alone. He didn't notice anything unusual and continued, "I was luckier. I spoke to the owner of the local restaurant. Heinz was here. Left in the afternoon."

They stood surrounded by thickening fog.

"I found out," Wirski continued, "that the tunnel to the north is about five kilometers from here. This place is a hole surrounded by mountains, a unique place to commit a crime, a perfect place to kill."

"But where could Heinz be now?" Father Sebastian asked.

"The study of this place should give us a clue," Stefan said. "Fact A—the train moves from north to south; fact B—they have selected Sterbfritz because it is located between the two tunnels. What's more, the tracks are in the valley, which is frequently foggy, causing poor visibility.

"Heinz must jump on the roof to enter the train, but he could not jump when the train is just about to enter the tunnel. He would be dead right away. This excludes the tunnel to the south," Stefan said. "He must be . . ."

"Sure," Father Sebastian interrupted. "I see, he jumps when the train leaves the tunnel, lies flat on the roof. In this fog nobody would spot him, not even the floodlights could penetrate it. Then, when the train is in the tunnel, he enters through a window."

"The train makes such a noise in the tunnel," Stefan said, "that even a shot cannot be heard."

"So Heinz must be," Father Sebastian said, "at the tunnel to the north. What are we waiting for? Let's go."

"All right," Wirski said. "I hope it is not too late."

The two men rushed to the car and drove north through the fog.

XXII

Midnight, November 8, 1942

Heinz had been alone in the bushy woods over the exit of the Sterbfritz tunnel for three hours. Most of that time it had been drizzling. Visibility was very bad, which he knew was both a disadvantage and an advantage. It required intense concentration to watch for an armored car in each train as it emerged from the tunnel. Heinz did not expect the train he was awaiting to be out right now. The earliest he could expect the Führer's special train would be midnight, but he watched every train from eleven o'clock on to sharpen his vision and to be ready.

The bad weather was an advantage to him because it hid him in the trees and bushes around him. He would feel almost invisible jumping on the train and climbing in the window.

Heinz had stopped that afternoon in the little café, Zum Adler, where he was able to get some food; he ate two dinners, gave the rest of his coupons to a drunken old man who haunted the café, and left for his hiding place.

When the midnight freight train filled the tunnel with thunder and sent echoes across the valley, he moved out of his hiding place and swiftly followed the path toward the ledge above the southern end of the tunnel. He dropped down onto the ledge, eased his body into the niche behind the overhanging vines, now nearly leafless, and became one with the dark mountain side. He checked his gear once more to help collect his wits in preparation for the long vigil.

He expected that the Führer's train should pass soon—it was one that did not have to keep to a timetable. His exultation was so great at finally being in place, poised for the act he had been planning for so long, that he did not feel the cold or suffer from the confinement of his rocky perch.

He began his meditation—a familiar ascent through love, horror, dread, and repulsion to rage. The images came effortlessly now; no longer a chaotic and paralyzing torrent, they were systematized by long practice, orchestrated until they had an almost supernatural clarity. Their purpose was to serve as implements of action. The faces of home, peace, childhood; the day of waiting against the stone wall of St. Stanislaw; watching old Bialy, the carter, cower and creep toward disgraceful death; the four black-clad men in the open car with death heads ostentatiously declaring their vocation and allegiance; the sickening, helpless waiting with hands bound; the paralysis and suffocation of lying in the heap of dead men, half-conscious, alive only to pain; the hurried surgery in the convent cellar; the belated knowledge of the cruel weeks of his mother's agony; the imagined screams, her pain, her degradation; then mass killings, unimaginable massacres, Lilka's mother herded with hundreds of others into a cattle car, then shot, gassed, tortured, or simply starved to death.

Images then of a man in uniform shouting victory and glory, blood and honor, salvation, his bent arm jerking up and down rigidly as though a spring in his puppet's soul worked a mechanism triggered by his disjointed words. A man whom bullets would not kill. Whose pomp and power extended over the face of Europe. Who held legions under his dominion sealed with the emblem of a death head, to perform unspeakable evil in his name. Heinz visualized the Führer's face, as he had sketched it in the museum. Like the Führer, Heinz gave himself over to rage, not unconditionally, but in practiced stages. He must relinquish sanity in order to have access to powers within himself that a sane man automatically rejects, as a sound body sloughs off invading disease. Powers that destroy their host. He let himself be permeated by fury, unreason. He made the last ascent to madness, in which he saw the act already accomplished, himself a murderer.

When he had reached the high plateau of serenity where his body was filled with reined-in strength and his mind was hard and sharp, empty of thought and image, he shifted his position infinitesimally, checked his watch, and looked out over the sodden countryside.

A slight wind stirred the trees; low gray clouds shut off the sky. Everything seemed a hallucination in the high state of exultation he had reached. The train rumbled beneath him, the smoke momentarily engulfed him, rattled the vines that curtained his hiding place. Only his purpose, his clear mind, and pounding blood were real. He fixed the image of his desire before him like a holy icon, with all his strength willing the future to become present—the ranting actor stilled, the hero dead. A clear, ringing ecstasy filled him like a shaft of sun falling on crystal in a dark room. He counted the cars.

As it drew near, all rage coiled deep inside him, out of the range of feeling; he flexed ankles, wrists, fingers, and crouched for the leap. He breathed deeply and rapidly, preparing his lungs to hold clear air. When the smoke curled up over the hillside, it would cover his descent over the ledge, his drop onto the train. The moment his fingers let go the stone ridge and his body hurled through the roaring, blinding void toward the moving train, all sense of his own being left him. As if in a dream, he heard a voice scream, "Adam, don't, don't jump." He must have imagined it, he thought. When he made contact with the car roof he was thrown off balance. In the darkness he grasped frantically for a hold. Before he stopped himself he was hanging off the side of the car. He pulled himself up and remained flat on the top of the train. He had to remain still. The searchlights from the amored cars in the front and rear of the train penetrated the drizzle and the smoke for a few moments, passing him; then the darkness covered his body again.

Heinz knew that it would take only minutes before the train reached the other tunnel, called the Sterbfritz tunnel, 1,093 meters long. Now the minutes appeared as eternity. He listened to every rattle, creak, and sound of the train. There was no change in its pace; he had not been spotted. The train barreled on into the night.

The clouds of sparks made it possible to see the outlines of the cars; at the front of the car just ahead he made out a window that seemed to be open a crack. He made his way over the car, crouching low. The window was narrow, but it slid down easily and locked in a halfway position. A glance inside showed the room to be a small lavatory. He put his feet in through the window, then slid down rapidly, holding on to the roof until only his arms remained outside.

He locked the window silently and pulled the revolver out of his side pocket. He freed the catch. With his left hand he touched the handle. He listened. The rhythm of the train was the only sound he could hear.

Heinz had waited for this moment during his sleepless nights and his daydreams. He knew now that he was only seconds away from the moment when he would face him and kill him.

Some shadows of the past took hold of him for another split second. Would Father Sebastian approve of his act? He saw his tired face. Then Lilka. The last time he saw her, she had wanted to tell him something. Did she want to tell him that she loved him? Could he still turn back? The train was now slowing its pace. He could still jump out undetected.

Then Else; could he ever face her again? Did he love her? But could he face another day with the knowledge that the man in whose name his father and he were executed was still alive? Heinz opened the door.

The man was alone, standing in a large salon, staring at a table covered with maps and diagrams. More maps were pinned to the walls. He was wearing glasses and only when he raised his head was Heinz sure it was the man he had come to kill, Adolf Hitler.

A look of horror, like a flash of recognition, crossed his face; he almost seemed to greet his assassin. Heinz pulled the trigger once, aiming at his chest. He heard the explosion of his shot. For a split second he saw the hate in the man's eyes. Heinz pulled the trigger again and again. The man gave a groan and doubled over. When the body fell to the floor, Heinz stood still. He fell into a sort of trance, jubilant at his success, unbelieving of his joy. It was several seconds before escape occurred to him.

Heinz retreated to the lavatory and closed the door behind him. He crawled through the window on to the roof of the car. As he was lying there, struggling for breath, the train began to slow down. Through the rattling and noise of the steel wheels on the tracks, Heinz discerned voices. Someone was shouting.

A wave of moist, cold air enveloped him. The train had just left the tunnel. It was still dark outside and it drizzled. Heinz planned to jump from the roof, then to disappear in the bushes. As his eyes adjusted to the objects around him, he found that they were crossing a high bridge. Heinz had to wait.

At that moment a beam of light shone from behind him. A voice shouted, "Halt! Halt!"

Heinz leaped forward. There was a shot but it missed. As Heinz ran forward he heard steps somewhere behind him. He reached the end of the car, jumped to the roof of the next one. The beam of the flashlight followed him. There was another shot and another miss. Heinz was still running and jumping. The train had just left the bridge. On the side of the tracks was a wide shoulder and behind it bushes and trees. Heinz was ready to jump down.

Suddenly a stream of floodlights opened on him. Heinz was facing a row of O's of K-78 rifles.

Heinz heard the salvo. He felt warm, joyful with the thought of Hitler's death. He was now in Polansk, a small boy. He saw his father smiling at him; his mother smiled, too. She took him into her arms.

Inside the train, Friedrich Cart of the MACABR unit if alive might regret his resemblance to the Führer.

EPILOGUE

Sunday, November 8, 1942

After the Führer's train left Fulda, it moved south for seven kilometers before it stopped.

It was four-fifteen in the morning; it was foggy and drizzling. Bormann, one of Hitler's close associates, came to the Führer's car and asked him to transfer to another train, waiting on the parallel track. Hitler became annoyed about this change. There had been an air attack on Berlin the previous evening and there was depressing news from various battle fronts. The Americans had landed in Africa, and the train was delayed because at each major station Hitler and his entourage listened to the news of the landing.

First, Hitler told Bormann that he did not want to move and wanted to know whose idiotic scheme this change of trains had been. Bormann replied that it had been planned by Obersturmbannführer Malec. Hitler asked Bormann to specify the reasons or to ask Malec to state them, to which Bormann replied that it was impossible since Malec had died that afternoon. Cause of death was an unexplained accident. Hitler was disturbed. He made the decision to accept Malec's plan. He crossed the tracks and boarded the other train, which followed the original one by ten minutes.

"We are fortunate, Mein Führer," Bormann said. "This was the last train from Berlin to have escaped the bombardment."

. . .

On a Sunday in April 1948 the boys of the Oberschule stood at attention in front of the school building. The mountains were still covered by snow, but the grass of the fields near the school had become green again. In the school garden the narcissus and hyacinths bloomed. The boys were called to attend a ceremony for the students of the school who had been the victims of Nazism.

Dr. Neufeind, the director of the school, read the names of those students, giving a short description of how each of them died. When he read the name of Heinz Hauptmann, he stopped for a moment.

After only a moment of silence he repeated "Heinz Hauptmann," adding that he had been born Adam Leski, and then he read the next name.

It was just as well since the boys had hoped that the ceremony would not last too long. They wanted to go to Nyphelheim to buy *Sacher, Linzer, or Pischinger* tarts and drink sweet Brazilian coffee. There they would form into rowdy groups; they would hang around the café and the bakery, never sated; they would return singing and shouting, pushing and punching along the road back to the Oberschule.